"That does it. I want you out of my car. Now."

Paige threw aside her blanket and leapt out of the front seat. She jerked open the back door and tugged on Cooper's arm.

Cooper had reached the limit of his patience. He yanked her toward him and settled her on his thigh. "Now," he told her in a controlled voice, "if you'll pipe down for a minute, I'll tell you what happened. I wasn't trying to hurt your hamster."

Her look was skeptical. "Then why were you reaching for him?"

"I wanted to scare him out of that blasted wheel."

"Henry loves that wheel. It's how he gets his exercise."

Cooper found her nearness fractured his concentration. "It, uh, makes enough noise to raise the dead. I don't see how you can sleep through it. I sure can't."

Paige's focus waivered. As Cooper held her gently, it was difficult to think of anything but how strong his arms were. And how it wouldn't be Henry that would keep them awake now....

Dear Reader,

It's May... it's springtime! Flowers are in bloom,
love is in the air... *and* on every page of this month's
Silhouette Romance selection.

Silhouette Romance novels always reflect the magic
of love in compelling stories that will make you
laugh and cry and move you time and time again.
This month is no exception. Our heroines find
happiness with the heroes of their dreams—from the
boy next door to the handsome, mysterious stranger.
We guarantee their heartwarming stories of love will
delight you.

May continues our WRITTEN IN THE STARS
series. Each month in 1992, we're proud to present a
book that focuses on the hero and his astrological
sign. This month we're featuring the stubborn,
protective Taurus man in the delightful *Rookie Dad*
by Pepper Adams.

In the months to come watch for Silhouette
Romance books by your all-time favorites such as
Diana Palmer, Suzanne Carey, Annette Broadrick,
Brittany Young and many, many more. The
Silhouette Romance authors and editors love to hear
from readers, and we'd love to hear from *you*.

Happy Springtime... and happy reading!

Valerie Susan Hayward
Senior Editor

TERRI LINDSEY

Going My Way

Silhouette Romance

Published by Silhouette Books New York

America's Publisher of Contemporary Romance

For Henry,
who covered a lot of long, hot miles with us,
and seldom complained.

SILHOUETTE BOOKS
300 E. 42nd St., New York, N.Y. 10017

GOING MY WAY

ISBN: 0-373-08865-5

First Silhouette Books printing May 1992

All the characters in this book have no existence outside the
imagination of the author and have no relation whatsoever to
anyone bearing the same name or names. They are not even
distantly inspired by any individual known or unknown to the
author, and all incidents are pure invention.

®: Trademark used under license and registered in the United
States Patent and Trademark Office and in other countries.

Printed in the U.S.A.

TERRI LINDSEY'S

experiences as a stockbroker taught her to expect the unexpected. "Like the time an angel-faced little grandmother came in," she recounts, "and announced she wanted to take advantage of a hot stock tip she'd received from a fellow poker player."

The one thing in Terri's life that was never unexpected, however, was that she would be a writer. As an adolescent she wrote for the entertainment of her family and friends. Today she writes for those who believe in that special bond between a man and a woman.

Terri lives with her husband and two dogs by a lake in Florida.

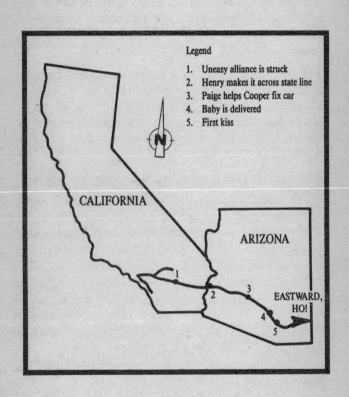

Legend

1. Uneasy alliance is struck
2. Henry makes it across state line
3. Paige helps Cooper fix car
4. Baby is delivered
5. First kiss

CALIFORNIA

ARIZONA

EASTWARD, HO!

Chapter One

A vulture coasted high on the desert thermals, its dark wings seeming not to move. Another bird joined the circling deathwatch, then another.

How long did it take to die of exposure in the desert? Paige Ruegger wondered as she watched the small gathering in the cloudless sky. Hours? Days?

With a shudder, she turned her attention back to the palm-size ball of fur panting in the cage she clutched on her lap. "We'll make it, Henry. Those nasty birds aren't after us," she assured the hamster. "It looks like they're at least a mile away."

But then, she'd already learned: in the desert, looks were often deceiving.

"They don't seem to be targeting us," she amended. *Yet.* Eager to change the subject, she promised, "When we get back to Florida, I'll get one of those clear plastic hamster palaces with all the tunnels and toys. And I'll give you cheese and cookies every day. Just hang in there, Henry,'' she pleaded.

Carefully, Paige set his cage on the driver's seat and walked around to the front of her car.

She had a perfectly good panel truck back home in Plymouth, Florida, and she wished for it now. Unfortunately what she was stuck with was this old gas-burner.

Arnold had meant well, bless his heart. When he'd dug the car out of the long-neglected shed and given it to her, he'd thought he was giving her a vehicle that would speed her back to Plymouth. Paige eyed the steam hissing out from under the radiator cap for the fourth time today. Maybe whatever was wrong with this monster was simple to fix. If only she knew something about cars! But her cousin kept their cars and trucks in working order.

The thought of Waldo Steinhauser released a painful wave of guilt and worry she'd been struggling to hold at bay. Everything was going to be all right, she told herself, swallowing hard. Maggie had said the doctor had told her Waldo was improving. *When I get home and can take care of him, everything will be all right. I'll never let him lift a monkey wrench or a bag of tree fern again.*

She hadn't reckoned on old age. *I should have,* she chastised herself. *I should never have gone to Tipilo.* But Waldo had seemed so energetic and strong when he'd waved her off on her way to California. It was easy to forget he was eighty-four.

Now he lay in a hospital in Florida while she was stuck almost three thousand miles away in the fiery Mojave Desert.

Paige came back and picked up Henry's cage. She slumped down on the front seat, car door open, and considered just giving in and letting the tears flow. It wouldn't help matters, but it might make her feel better.

The vultures came to mind.

On the other hand, she might need all the moisture she could retain.

The brown and white hamster lay panting on the bottom of his cage. "Hang in there, Henry," Paige coaxed, feeling more than a little desperate.

Carefully she relocated Henry's cage outside, in the patch of shade provided by the car. It wasn't much of an improvement, but it was the best she could do. She picked up the road map and gently fanned the hamster.

"Is that better?" she murmured, studying him anxiously. "As soon as the radiator cools off a little bit, I'll fill it with water. Then we can be on our way."

Until the next time the car overheated.

Captain Cooper Angelsmith, United States Marine Corps, stared at the gas gauge of his rented car in impotent fury. If this had been *his* car, the damned thing would have been accurate. But his car lay in pieces in a rented bay at Sim's Automotive in Oceanside.

He'd planned to spend his week of leave rebuilding the engine of his 1964 Morgan Plus 4. He hadn't anticipated the need to drive across the country. But then, he hadn't expected to find his bank accounts drained and his credit cards rejected.

Nathan. It had to be Nathan. Only his younger brother had access to every savings account, checking account and credit card Cooper owned. When he'd arrived at Camp Pendleton four months ago and opened them, it seemed the prudent thing to do, seeing Nathan was his partner in Cooper's Classics, his antique and classic car rebuilding business. If something happened to Cooper, Nathan could access his brother's funds. Instead something had happened to the money, leaving Cooper high and dry and Nathan mysteriously elusive.

Cooper recalled the humiliation of being refused his ticket to Jacksonville, North Carolina, at the airline desk.

Thank God one oil company card had still been good. He'd used it to rent this little gem, then had headed toward Jacksonville, home of the soon-to-be-late Nathan Angelsmith. He'd even found this desert road, thinking he could circumvent the ponderous I-10 Friday traffic.

Then his luck had run out, leaving him stranded, surrounded by miles of baking sand, cacti, and Joshua trees. The traffic on *this* road wasn't heavy at all. In fact, in the past thirty minutes, it had been nonexistent.

He caught a movement out of the corner of his eye and turned to look.

In the distance, three vultures wheeled in the seared blue sky.

"Hi, fellas," he muttered. "Find a tasty motorist?" Cooper watched the dark birds for a minute longer, then flung open his door and got out to double-check the fuel tank.

He had to get to Jacksonville before his business and all his assets vanished as neatly as his brother had.

Paige watched with trepidation as the shiny RV lumbered off the highway to pull in front of her car. Slowly she stood, brushing sand from her jeans. She should be relieved and elated, she thought, trying to quiet her uneasiness. Someone kind enough to stop deserved better than suspicion. Still, she'd heard about the weirdos that combed the desert, preying on the unfortunate.

On the other hand, the driver of the RV was taking a risk, too. For all he knew, a drug-crazed motorcycle gang could be lurking behind her car.

Paige managed a grateful smile. The smile grew when the occupants of the RV proved to be an older couple. She guessed them to be in their mid-sixties.

"Hello, dear," the woman said, offering her hand. "I'm Edna Butterworth, and this is my husband, Stan. It appears you have some car trouble."

Paige shook hands with Stan and Edna. "Paige Ruegger. My car overheat—"

Her words died as a tall man with hard eyes got out of the RV.

Edna turned to follow Paige's gaze. "Cooper, come over here, dear. Paige, this is Cooper Angelsmith. He ran out of gas, and we're taking him into Indio with us."

Ran out of gas? What kind of idiot would allow himself to run out of gas in the Mojave Desert? Paige noticed the color creep up his neck to stain his high, broad cheekbones, thinking she'd be embarrassed, too, if she'd done something that stupid.

"The gas gauge doesn't work," he said, his words clipped, as if he hated explaining. "Rental car."

Paige nodded politely.

Without another word, Cooper walked to her car and began checking under the open hood. With a rag, he twisted off the radiator cap, stepping back as a geyser of steam escaped. When it cleared, he bent closer. And scowled. "Do you have water?"

"Yes," Paige answered. "I was just about to—"

"We've got some," Stan said, emerging from the RV with a gallon jug of water. He poured almost half of it into the radiator. The two men discussed the situation for a moment, then Cooper dropped the hood into place. Wiping his hands on the rag, he approached the women.

"The radiator's a mess. Looks like someone had a field day with a soldering gun."

With a sinking feeling, Paige knew whatever he was talking about was bound to cost her time or money. She had little of either. "Which means . . . ?"

"Your engine is water-cooled. Air flowing through the radiator cools the water that keeps the engine from overheating when it's running. This radiator is welded in so many places it's hard for air to get through, so your engine overheats."

"Why would someone weld a radiator?" asked Paige, battling despair.

"Leaks," Stan supplied. "The car is well over fourteen years old, and this is probably the original radiator. Whoever welded it was likely trying to make it last as long as possible."

Arnold had probably forgotten about the true condition of the radiator years ago.

"If you drive slowly and carry water with you, you can make the thing last a while longer," Cooper told her.

"And if I don't drive slowly?" She had to get back to Florida quickly. What if Waldo stopped improving? He might ask for her and she wouldn't be there for him.

There wasn't *time* to drive slowly.

He shrugged. "Then you overheat."

Paige swallowed the tears that threatened, refusing to reveal her desperation to strangers, no matter how wellmeaning. "How—how much would a new radiator cost, do you think?"

"Out here?" Cooper glanced out at the desert that stretched around them. "The sky's the limit."

She released a pent-up, discouraged sigh. "Water it is."

Edna patted Paige's shoulder and smiled encouragingly. "You're hot and tired, dear. Why don't we follow you into Indio? There's a nice little diner there that serves homemade pie. It'll be our treat. Afterward, maybe Cooper would be good enough to give your car one more check before you continue on your way." The older woman raised her eyes to Cooper.

He gave a single, chopped nod of agreement.

"There? You see?" she continued to Paige. "Everything is taken care of."

Paige wanted to protest her rescuers had done enough already, but she was too relieved at having the security of someone close by if her car acted up again. "Thank you, Mrs. Butterworth. I appreciate your help."

"Please call me Edna. It's much more comfortable, don't you think?"

As she drove into Indio, Paige was relieved no one had suggested Cooper ride with her. There was something about the man that made her...well, *uncomfortable*. When he stood next to her she felt a certain electric awareness of him. He was tall and lean, and his golden-brown hair was conservatively cut but long enough to tempt feminine fingers. His eyes were the dark amber of Kentucky bourbon. She imagined they'd be devastating to the woman who saw them filled with laughter. Or desire.

Paige straightened in her seat. "It must be the heat, Henry," she muttered. "My brain is turning to mush."

She slowed the car when Stan motioned he wanted to pull ahead of her, and Paige followed him to a restaurant with "Norma's" scrawled in pink neon across the large front window.

The place must have good food, Paige thought, because the asphalt lot was crowded. She found a parking place, then got out of the car, taking Henry in his cage with her.

Cooper eyed the cage curiously, but remained silent.

"What have we here?" Stan asked.

"I can't leave Henry in the car. It's too hot for him," Paige explained.

Edna peered at the ball of brown and white fur huddled in a nest of wood shavings. "What is, uh, Henry?"

"A hamster."

Edna's head snapped up. "Isn't a hamster a lot like a...*mouse?*" she asked.

"More like a rat," Cooper muttered.

Edna's eyes widened.

"He is *not* like a rat." Paige shot Cooper a scorching glare. Rats were nasty and sly. Henry was cute and crafty.

Cooper's mouth twitched at the corner.

Stan put his arm around his wife and drew her away from her fixed study of the hamster. "Edna, hamsters are perfectly harmless. They aren't mice, or rats." He smiled at Paige. "I don't think Norma would appreciate a, er, *pet* in her restaurant. Why don't you take Henry to the gas station next door? Tell Larry I sent you. His office is air-conditioned, and I'm sure he won't mind if you leave a quiet, little hamster there for an hour. Cooper, why don't you go with her?"

"That's okay," Paige said hastily. "It won't take me a minute. I'll meet you in the restaurant."

Inside the station, Paige knocked on the door with the frosted glass window, and a man's voice invited her into the cool office. The drop in temperature felt wonderful. Paige introduced herself to the owner, Larry Jones, and explained the situation.

He was fascinated. "Don't recall ever hamster-sitting before."

"I appreciate it, Larry. This desert heat has been hard on Henry." She walked to the door, preparing to re-enter the furnace that was the Mojave. "Please don't open the cage," Paige cautioned. "Hamsters are master escape artists."

The wiry little man with leatherlike skin nodded and shooed her out. "Don't you worry. I've got better things to do with my time than mess with the likes of that critter. He'll be safe.''

She found her rescuers seated in a booth under a wagon-wheel hanging lamp. The only space left was on the banquette, next to Angelsmith. With a smile she hoped didn't look as forced as it felt, Paige slid into place, careful not to get any closer to him than she had to.

It was pleasant to sit in the cool of the air-conditioned restaurant, listening to the low hum of conversation and the clink of flatware against dishes. After so many miles with only Henry to talk to, human company was welcome. She glanced up at Cooper's handsome profile. Straight, short nose. Prominent cheekbones. Strong, square jaw...

On the other hand, Henry was a very good listener.

"So, Paige," Stan said, laying down his menu, "are you taking in the sights of the Southwest, or are you just passing through on your way to someplace else?"

"Just passing through."

As if sensing her hesitation to discuss her plans and destination with near strangers, Edna smiled and volunteered, "Stan and I live here in Indio. We moved here from Atlantic City five years ago when Stan retired from the postal service." She beamed at her husband. "Thirty years. He was the best letter carrier in New Jersey."

Stan reddened and patted his wife's hand. His pleased embarrassment charmed Paige.

"Cooper, you said you're a captain in the Marine Corps," Edna continued. "Where are you headed, dear?" she asked him.

Before he could answer, the waitress appeared, complete with brown polyester uniform and red gingham neckerchief. She took their orders and left.

"Now, you were telling us where you're headed," prompted Edna.

"North Carolina." He toyed with a corner of his paper place mat. "Jacksonville, North Carolina."

"Jacksonville." It sounded like Stan was turning the name over in his mind. "That anywhere near Camp Lejeune?"

"Yes, sir. Jacksonville is right outside the base."

Stan grinned. "My brother was stationed there when he was in the marines. That's where my oldest nephew was born. You stationed there?"

Paige couldn't see in Cooper any evidence of impatience with Stan's friendly curiosity. Why, then, did she have the impression the marine was anxious to be gone?

"I'm stationed at Camp Pendleton." At Stan and Edna's blank looks he added, "Near Oceanside. California."

"Ah! North of San Diego."

The waitress brought their orders—slices of fresh, homemade pie all around. It had been years since Paige had eaten cherry pie that hadn't come out of a supermarket freezer. Both Butterworths had selected coconut cream. She glanced at Cooper's plate. Apple pie. Why didn't that surprise her?

"Are you a student, Paige?" Edna asked.

Bless you, Edna Butterworth. Paige knew she looked younger than her twenty-five years, but not *that* much younger. "I'm in the nursery business. I grow orchids."

"Oh, how exciting!" Edna exclaimed. "Orchids are so exotic."

Paige smiled. "Yes, they do have the reputation of being exotic, don't they?" So exotic the early Greeks had named them *orchis*—testicle. Doubtless the designation was due to the shape of the enlarged tubers of many orchids, but the grace and beauty of the flowers' petals and their often sweet fragrance had long ago convinced Paige orchids were more the embodiment of femininity.

Stan pushed his empty plate away. "Edna tried growing them once, but she didn't have any luck."

"Oh? What kind?"

The older woman thought a minute. "Sim...sim..." She gave Paige a look of apology. "I have trouble with the names. It was sim something."

"Cymbidium?"

"That's it. Sim what-you-said. Oh, it was so lovely when I bought it in San Francisco. After I got it back to Indio and hung it in my kitchen window it went into a decline. I was so careful to water it and feed it, but it died anyway."

"I'm not surprised. A cymbidium needs temperatures no higher than seventy degrees. You might have better luck with a phalaenopsis."

Edna started to jot the name down on her napkin, but stopped and looked at her in question.

"A moth orchid," Paige supplied.

"Thank you, dear. I'll remember that."

Paige made a mental note to send Edna Butterworth a couple of the plants when she got back to Florida.

Twenty minutes later, Edna and Stan's address scrawled on a scrap of paper tucked in her purse, Paige said her heartfelt thank-yous and her good-byes. The Butterworths were effusive and reassuring. Angelsmith gave her a short nod.

She walked directly to the gas station. Larry was in the garage working under a car up on one of the two hydraulic racks.

"Come to get your little buddy?" he asked, giving her a friendly grin. "You know where he is."

"Thanks, Larry. Would you mind if I used your office phone? It's a collect call."

"Sure, go right ahead."

Paige stepped into the cool dimness of the office, and closed the door behind her. Henry's travel cage was where she'd left it.

Quickly she dialed her neighbor's number. Maggie Umstead answered on the first ring.

"Thank God you called!" cried the seventy-one-year-old after Paige greeted her. "Girl, don't you worry about Waldo. He's still in intensive care, but he's improvin'. It's just... There's another problem." She paused. "I just found out the sheriff posted your property weeks ago. They're sayin' you haven't paid your taxes in over two years. The county's goin' to auction off your land, your house, your office, your greenhouses—everything—in nine days."

The room swayed around Paige. Blindly she groped for the armrest, and eased herself down into the old wooden swivel chair. Was it possible Waldo hadn't paid their taxes? Their land was going up for auction. She sat there stunned, unbelieving.

"Paige?" Maggie sounded worried. "I know you've got enough on your mind, what with Waldo in the hospital and all. I went through Waldo's office, tryin' to find your bank book, or checkbook—*somethin'* to ship you so you could get those taxes paid. All I found were a couple of money orders. One was made out to Florida Power Corporation, and the other was to the telephone company."

Money orders? Why would Waldo use money orders? "Keep looking, Maggie. There has to be a checkbook there somewhere. Waldo wouldn't use money orders on a regular basis. There must have been a foul-up with the bank for him to do that."

Waldo had always insisted on taking care of paying their bills. He'd lived through the Depression, losing his money and farm when his bank failed. Now he was a fanatic about debt. Knowing his history, Paige had conceded when he'd claimed the position of bookkeeper. Maybe the task had been too much for him.

"Every inch," Maggie was saying. "I went over every inch of your house and the office. Thought I'd at least find somethin' at Enchanted Orchids. Nothin'. No checkbook. No bank statement. Forty dollars cash in a coffee can, is all. Want me to send it to you?"

"Keep it for my phone calls."

"You know I'd pay the taxes for you, Paige, if I had the money." The faint quiver in the old woman's voice revealed her distress.

"I know you would, Maggie. We'll get through this, don't you worry. Waldo will recover and tell you where to find the checkbook. Meanwhile, I'll get home as soon as I can. I'm having a little car trouble, nothing I can't handle. I wish I was there with you so you wouldn't worry so. Soon. I'll be home soon."

"Don't you worry about me, girl. I'll hold down the fort till you get here. You drive carefully, now, y'hear?"

Paige plowed back her hair with shaking fingers. "I hear." After she hung up, she stared up at the ceiling, blinking rapidly.

She could lose Waldo, her home and her business before she made it back to Plymouth.

That thought brought a wrenching twist in her middle. Fat tears splashed down her cheeks. She moved to Henry's cage and sat back on her heels, seeking comfort in the sight of him, in the familiar smell of well-tended hamster and regularly changed wood shavings.

Paige watched him running in his squeaky treadwheel. "Just because it's dim in here doesn't mean it's night, Henry. If you play in your wheel now, you'll be too tired to later."

Henry waddled to the side of the cage and sniffed the morsel of pie crust she offered him. He took it from her and stuffed it in his cheek pouch.

"Sorry I couldn't bring you any of the cherries. They probably aren't good for hamsters anyway." With a rumpled tissue she wiped the tears from her face and blew her nose. She closed her fingers around the cage handle. "C'mon. We can't stay in here forever."

She heard a man's voice call a greeting to Larry as the newcomer entered the garage. Halfway to a standing position, Paige froze. That voice was familiar.

"Larry Jones? Hello. I'm Cooper Angelsmith. Thought you might be looking for a good mechanic."

She couldn't say why she didn't just walk out of the office. Paige only knew she didn't want to make her presence known. Quietly she slid back into the chair behind Larry's battered metal desk, knowing the window's frosted glass would conceal her.

Paige envisioned Larry wiping his hands on a rag. "Well," he said, "I've already got one good mechanic—me. Got a good part-time mechanic, too. Not enough business to add another, leastwise not now. Sorry."

"Do you know of anyone looking for a mechanic?"

"Got you own tools?" Larry asked.

There was a faint pause. "No."

"Can't help you then. Mac needs a man with his own tools."

Another pause. Paige thought Cooper must have given one of his short nods. "Thanks, anyway."

What was Angelsmith doing out in the garage asking Larry for a job? He'd said he was on his way to Jacksonville. She'd sensed he was in a hurry.

She counted to fifty, enough time for Cooper to get out the door, but not enough for him to get so far away he wouldn't be willing to check her car one more time. Just a quick check.

Paige took up the cage, and walked out of the office. She waved at Larry. "Thanks!"

He smiled at her. "Any time."

She strode quickly out of the garage, after Angelsmith. "Cooper! Wait up!"

He stopped and looked over his shoulder. He didn't turn to face her, but waited for her to catch up.

"Do you have a minute to check my car?" she asked.

His eyes flickered to the hamster cage then back to her face, and Paige wondered if he knew she'd listened to his conversation with Larry Jones.

"A minute, yes."

In silence they returned to the restaurant parking lot.

Cooper raised the hood. "Start the car."

The inside of the car was like an oven set at full heat. A wall of hot air hit her in the face, stealing her breath.

"Today, if you please," Cooper rumbled.

Paige bristled. "He's a real Mr. Charm," she muttered to Henry. She stabbed her key into the ignition and turned it, applying a little pressure to the gas pedal.

Nothing happened.

She tried again. This time she got a thin *bizt*. Clunk.

Again she turned the key. *Bizt*. Clunk.

Paige gripped the steering wheel with both hands, the tendons standing out in her wrists. Sweat ran down her arms. Couldn't *anything* go right? At this rate she'd never make it back to Florida.

She leaned out through the open door. "It won't start."

"I can see that."

She bit down on her irritation and got out to stand beside him, watching as he touched this, probed that. "What's wrong with it?"

"It could be a couple of things," he said without looking up. "My guess is it's the starter, but I can't do anything without my tools."

Cooper wiped his forearm across his forehead. He wished for his tools, stored neatly in their chest back at Sim's in Oceanside. Life would be better still if he had his car, his bank accounts, and all his credit cards in working order. Cash in his pocket would be nice, too. Instead his last credit card had been rejected when he'd called to rent another car. He thumped his fist against the fender and cursed under his breath. He wanted to crush something in his bare hands—something like his brother's will to live.

Nathan was a dead man. His life span would extend exactly as long as it took Cooper to get to Jacksonville.

Which, at the moment, looked like a very long time.

"I have a few tools," Paige volunteered. "They were in the trunk when I got the car. They're in kind of crummy condition."

"Like the car."

Paige opened her mouth to protest, but couldn't quite bring herself to give voice to such an obvious lie. He was right. The car was in crummy condition. But she was lucky to have a car at all.

She had no intention of revealing her penury to Cooper Angelsmith. "Gee, I wish I'd bought that Cadillac," she said flippantly.

Cooper directed his gaze down the length of her body, and slowly back up. Paige felt as if warm bourbon had been poured over her naked skin.

"So do I," he said, his voice deep and rich with suggestion.

Heat scoured her face. "Can you fix the car?" She hated asking him for anything. Being broke was hell.

Cooper had had enough. He had problems of his own. His first concern was to find a way to make enough money to get across the country. He needed transportation.

An idea flashed and took hold. Reluctantly Cooper examined the angles. He walked around the car, inspecting it. The thing was as big as a battle cruiser, dinged and rusted, but if he could get it working again, it would qualify as transportation. At least it should get him out of the desert, back to civilization where it would be easier to catch a fast ride east.

With her T-shirt emblazoned with Apopka Foliage Festival, and her utilitarian jeans and sneakers, Paige Ruegger didn't exactly look as if she was rolling in money. He doubted she could afford many auto repairs, which is probably what it would take to keep the crate going. She needed someone who could fix her car.

She needed him.

Chapter Two

"Let me see the tools," he said.

Quickly, Paige stepped forward with her keys. The trunk opened with a screech. She reached inside and dragged forward a cardboard box, brushing the flaps back to reveal a jumble of old screwdrivers, a few rusted wrenches, a lathe and a corroded measuring tape.

He picked through the assortment. Junk. Useless junk for his purposes. The few items he might be able to use looked like they'd crumble in his hands if put to work.

Paige's pretty face was filled with such hope Cooper didn't like having to meet her eyes. Ruthlessly he shut down on that response. He couldn't afford to waste another minute on her and her damn car.

"What are you kids still doing here?" Stan called as he and Edna crossed the parking lot on their way to their RV. "We thought you'd be off to conquer the world by now." He peered under the hood, then looked at Cooper. "Don't tell me, let me guess. It needs more water."

"More like a new starter," Cooper said.

"It won't turn over? Could it be the battery? I've got jumper cables."

For an instant Cooper gritted his teeth with impatience. Then he accepted the inevitable. The Butterworths were kind, decent people who had helped him. He would go through the motions even though he was certain the problem wasn't the battery. "Let's give it a try."

They hooked the cables from the idling RV to Paige's car. She tried unsuccessfully to start the engine.

"That narrows it down to the starter, the alternator, or the generator," Stan said, folding the cables, then replacing them in the RV's storage compartment.

Edna looked thoughtful. During the attempt to get Paige's car going, she'd studied the car, then Cooper, then Paige. What was going through her mind? Paige wondered.

As if in answer to that unspoken question, Edna drew Paige away from the men with a guiding hand.

"Now, dear," she said in a soft but no-nonsense tone of voice, "where are you going?"

"Florida." Just saying it was like pulling the plug from a straining dike. Desperation swept through her. "I *have* to get back home, Edna. My cousin had a heart attack and he's in the hospital. He's my only relative!" Paige couldn't bring herself to mention the taxes. Added to Waldo's condition, this latest calamity was still too fresh, too raw. She couldn't think about it now. "I'm—I'm all he's got," she confided raggedly. "I have to get back right away. He needs me."

Edna put her arm around Paige's shoulders and gave her a little hug. "And here's your opportunity. It's obvious to me Cooper's in a hurry to get to Jacksonville. Haven't you sensed it? That man needs you, dear. Think about it. He could keep your car running in exchange for the lift. And it wouldn't be a bad thing to have such a strapping young man along for protection."

Paige assessed Cooper from under her lashes. "Yeah? Who's going to protect me from *him?* A *marine.*"

"Yes, they do have rather racy reputations where women are concerned," Edna mused. "But Cooper seems like such a nice young man. A little too serious, perhaps, but that's not bad. Besides, such reputations are generally exaggerated. I suppose it's all part of that *machismo* thing. But it's up to you, dear." Paige searched Edna's face, torn by uncertainty. The woman was clearly serious. And her suggestion made an unpleasant sort of sense.

Paige studied Cooper again. He might be blunt and irritating, but she didn't think he was a mad slasher. Weren't mad slashers supposed to be pleasant and agreeable, lulling their intended victims' wariness? Assuming the handsome Marine Corps captain was innocent of lethal intentions, having someone along capable of making necessary car repairs could be her salvation.

"He doesn't have the tools he needs for repairs."

A satisfied light glimmered in Edna's eyes. "I'll talk to Stan. He has every tool known to man."

Cooper regarded the women with growing frustration. Wasting time, that's what he was doing. Wasting time that would be better spent looking for a job that would earn him enough money for a bus ticket. How long would it take him to scrape enough together for the fare? A week? Two weeks? He bunched a fist in frustration. Too long.

"You could help that little girl," said Stan in a low-pitched voice. "It's clear to see she needs you. If you help her, you'll help yourself, too. Paige needs your know-how, and you need her car. You keep her car running, you'll have a ride. You'll both get where you're going."

Cooper turned his head in time to see Paige turn back to Edna. He took stock of the young woman. Shoulder-length, blunt-cut hair the color of wild honey. Wide-spaced blue eyes. A shape that . . . well, definitely negative on the "little girl." A man could have a worse traveling companion.

"I don't have the tools and parts to get this junker running, and to keep it running," he said.

Stan directed a level look at Cooper. "I'll lend you tools. But I want them back when you get to Jacksonville."

Tools were expensive. "Why are you doing this?"

Stan smiled. "Three years ago our granddaughter, Sara, ran away from home. She called once, scared and broke, afraid to say where she was. Edna and I did everything we could to find that child, but turned up nothing. Last week she called from the bus station in Farenville, Idaho. A wonderful couple had fed her and bought her a bus ticket. Every day we thank God for the generosity of those people. They sent our granddaughter safely home to us. Edna and I will be happy if what we've done today helps you and Paige on your individual ways."

Edna urged Paige back to where the men stood, and the older couple acted as mediators in the arrangement.

Paige agreed to finance the trip. Cooper agreed to earn his way by keeping the car running, and acting as protector-in-general. That last part was Edna and Stan's idea, and it brought a flush to Paige's face. Cooper agreed, but she didn't like the arrogant smile that accompanied his assent.

"I want references," she insisted, panic setting in. "I want to talk to his commanding officer."

"You can talk to anyone *but* my commanding officer," Cooper said flatly, taking the matter out of the mediators' hands. "Talk to my sergeant. If anyone knows me, he does."

"No."

Cooper scowled. He leaned down to bring his face almost nose to nose with Paige. "Listen, sugar," he growled in an undertone, "you need me as much as I need your car. Don't push it. I'm not about to let you humiliate me in front of my superior officer. *Talk to my sergeant.*"

Paige glared at him, furious that his close proximity unnerved her. She steeled herself against the urge to step back. "No. Your sergeant might be afraid of you. Your commanding officer won't be."

"My sergeant knows me better than my commanding officer. And anyone who knows Sergeant Caudill knows he doesn't pull any punches. I don't have anything to hide."

Looking directly into Cooper's eyes, Paige said, "*I* don't know Sergeant Caudill. It's your C.O. or the deal's off." She knew she was bluffing. She hoped he didn't.

He said softly, "I can always hitchhike."

She wanted to tell him to do just that. She wanted to laugh in his face and walk away.

She wanted to get home.

Paige stared at Cooper for several seconds, struggling to swallow her frustration. *Think of Waldo, of Maggie.*

"All right," she said through clenched jaws. "What's your sergeant's number?"

It was dusk by the time Cooper finished installing the rebuilt starter Paige had bought from Larry. Actually, it was the second starter. After Cooper had installed the first one, he'd discovered it was defective. By that time the Butterworths had gone home.

Paige was hot, sticky, and bored. She wasn't qualified to do more than hand Cooper the tools he asked for, fetch cool water for them, and fan Henry. She had, however, obtained directions that would lead them to food and a place to stay the night. She dreaded breaking the news to Cooper of just how little money they had to travel across the country on.

After he returned the tools to their case, Cooper picked up the clean rag Paige handed him and began rubbing the car grease from his face, hands, and arms. "God," he sighed, "I want a shower, a meal, and a bed in an air-conditioned room. Maybe tomorrow we can get through the day without the transmission or something falling out."

Involuntarily, Paige moved a step away from him, pretending to check on Henry. She didn't think Cooper was going to like this. She knew she should have told him earlier what kind of budget constrictions they'd be forced to endure. Her only excuse was desperation.

"Have you made arrangements for rooms yet?" he asked. "I need to wash up before we go to dinner. This stuff just isn't coming off."

"I've reserved a place for us to stay the night," she hedged.

Cooper stopped rubbing and looked at her sharply. "What sort of 'place'? Is it air-conditioned?"

If they rolled the car windows down, the hot breeze off the Mojave could blow through. "Sort of."

He threw the rag into the trunk and pinned her with a warning look. "Does this place have running water?"

There were faucets in the communal rest rooms. "In a manner of speaking."

A muscle jumped in his jaw. "Just where do you plan for us to stay?" he asked, his voice deceptively mild.

Paige muttered her answer.

"Louder," he ordered.

"A campground outside of town."

Cooper stared at her in disbelief. She'd promised to finance the trip if he kept the car running. He'd just spent the last three hours laboring in hundred-degree weather keeping his end of the bargain. Now, by God, she'd keep hers.

"A *campground?* I just busted my butt replacing your starter in this parking lot from hell, and you expect me to spend the night at a campground? Sugar, I've already put in my time in a tent. I'm not a masochist. I don't like it. Now hustle your cute little fanny over to the restaurant telephone and get us *rooms* somewhere."

Paige looked down at Henry curled up in a brown and white furry ball. She longed to take him out and hold him, touch him to her cheek. Instead she forced herself to meet Cooper's angry gaze. She took a deep breath and let it out.

"There isn't enough money for us to stay at a motel, or even to eat dinner in a restaurant. I said I'd finance the trip, and I will. But that means sleeping in the car at campgrounds and buying our food at grocery stores. That's the only way we'll have enough for gas and parts—" she gestured toward the automobile "—assuming nothing serious goes wrong with this thing. I—I'm sorry if you expected better. I wish I had more money so we could travel more comfortably. But I don't."

Cooper commanded her gaze for a brutal moment longer, then abruptly turned toward the car. He raked his fingers through his hair. "All right. Let's get this show on the road." He faced her, the hardness in his expression stopping her as she bent to pick up Henry's cage. "But let's get one thing clear." He stabbed a blunt-tipped finger in her direction. "You weren't straight with me, sugar, and I don't like it."

Paige's hackles went up. She had enough to worry about without having to humor this big, bad marine. "I said I'd pay for the trip, but I never claimed we'd be staying at five-star hotels along the way. If I had a lot of money I wouldn't have agreed to saddle myself with you, would I? And *don't* call me sugar."

Something other than fury glittered in his amber eyes. "So you've agreed to 'saddle' yourself with me? Maybe this trip won't be so bad after all." He shut the trunk. "Sugar."

"I am *not* going to help you smuggle that tailless rat into this supermarket." Cooper's jawline took on a rigidity that spoke of strong-willed resistance.

Paige fixed him with an unwavering stare. "Oh, yes you are. No hamster, no food."

"Taking that thing in there is against the law."

"I doubt it. It might be against local health regulations, but against the law? No. Where does it say in the Constitution that hamsters don't have the right to live? You know Henry would die if we left him in the car."

"No loss," Cooper muttered.

Paige glared at him. "Not to you, maybe, but it would be a loss to me. A big loss."

"The temperature's dropping."

"Not enough." Paige refused to give an inch.

Cooper rolled his eyes. "Oh, hell, all right. The last thing I need is an hysterical woman on my hands. Especially one whining about her dead pet rat."

He got out of the car and waited while Paige picked up her purse and the hamster cage, then checked to make certain the car was locked.

"Now," she said, "you just walk close in front of me, and I'll camouflage the cage with my purse. Get a cart and head directly to the snack section. A couple of bags of cheese curls will hide Henry."

Cooper sullenly regarded the hamster. "I don't like cheese curls."

"Potato chips, then, or pretzels. Whatever, *just get going.*"

Cooper arched a warning eyebrow before he complied.

Paige knew they looked odd when they caravanned through the store's automatic doors, but as soon as that blessed cool air hit her she forgot about everything but the cessation of heat.

"Do you know how ridiculous we look?" Cooper demanded in an undertone. "Siamese twins joined by a big red purse. It's not bad enough I'm covered with grease and sweat."

"Well, I don't like it any better than you," Paige returned. "And I'd appreciate it if you'd stay down-draft of me."

Cooper's head snapped around. "Just remember how I got that way."

"Oh, I do. Sitting in the desert in a car you let run out of gas."

He stopped, and Paige ran into the back of him, jostling Henry's cage. "I told you," Cooper said through clenched teeth, "the fuel gauge was *broken.* The car was a rental."

"Okay, okay," she soothed impatiently, "the gauge was broken."

As soon as they reached the snack section, Paige snatched up two one-pound bags of cheese curls and leaned them against Henry's cage, now in the child seat of the cart. Cooper immediately replaced one of the curls with pretzels.

After pushing the cart up and down almost every aisle in the store, they added fruit, bottled water, powdered lemonade, and the fixings for sandwiches.

Getting through the checkout lane proved to be a miracle of modern choreography. At this hour, when most people were home eating dinner, the store was relatively empty, the lines short. Just before Cooper and Paige reached the register, she lifted Henry's cage and whisked it behind her large tote purse, which she slipped over Cooper's shoulder to rest in front of him. She nudged the cage under his arm. Then, smiling widely, she reached into the tote and got her wallet.

She had to hand it to Cooper. He was being cool about it. To look at his face one would never suspect he held a hamster under his arm.

The woman in line behind Cooper tried to peer around him to see what was going on.

"It's okay," he whispered to her. "We're with the store. We're conducting a test." He gave her a conspiratorial wink, then raised a finger to his lips in a gesture requesting her silence.

The shopper's eyebrows lifted, and she shaped an O with her mouth. With a smile, she settled back to watch.

Paige observed the exchange with amazement. Charm. Humor. This was a side of Cooper she hadn't seen before, a side she hadn't known existed.

The cashier finished ringing up their groceries and Paige handed over precious dollars. She piled the food into bags before a bag boy could arrive, and she and Cooper hurried out the door.

They reached the campgrounds and checked in with no problems. Following the manager's instructions, they found their space, which, to Paige's relief, was located near the rest rooms.

"Go wash up. I'll stay with the car," Cooper offered.

Paige suddenly found herself uneasy about leaving this difficult man alone with her car. He was clever, he could hot-wire it. Just how well did she really know this guy? Could she trust him?

"No, I know how much you want to get clean. You go first." She gave him her best winning smile.

Cooper glanced down to rub at a stain on his arm. "Afraid I'll steal the behemoth?" he asked. He looked up again. A sly grin spread over his mouth when he saw her face. "Give me a little credit, will you? If I were going to steal a car it wouldn't be this one. Maybe that blue number we passed coming in—four-wheel drive, decent gas mileage... air-conditioning."

Paige regarded Cooper narrowly. "You think you're so smart, don't you?"

Cooper's satisfied expression resembled that of a cat who'd just swallowed the prize canary. "I *am* smart." His smile faded. "Usually."

Paige took the flashlight out of the glove compartment. It had been Arnold's inspiration, rummaged from a junk drawer in his workshop. She hoped it worked. She didn't relish making the trip to the rest rooms and back in the dark. With a flick of her thumb she pressed the button. A pale beam revealed a disgruntled hamster. Quickly she turned it off.

"Do you have another flashlight?" Cooper asked.

"Uh, no." Paige felt selfish.

"I see. So I get to sit in the dark while you toddle off to the ladies' room."

Irritation overcame guilt. Didn't this guy ever stop griping? "I don't see any way around that. When I get back, you can toddle off to the men's room, and *I'll* sit in the dark. Happy?"

Cooper didn't grace her question with a reply. Instead he folded his arms, closed his eyes and settled back in the plastic-covered seat.

Moonlight washed over him, illuminating planes and angles of his face, neck and shoulders, drawing a pen-and-ink picture of a powerful male.

She wasn't immune to the aura of confident virility that surrounded him. She guessed he was a man used to being in charge. A man accustomed to being obeyed by other men. And with women—

Paige grabbed her train case and towel and hastened off to the women's rest room.

It was safer not to speculate about that man. Her imagination was too fertile.

She didn't even *like* Cooper Angelsmith.

Just when she thought she had the man pegged, he tricked her by doing something nice. Like making their sandwiches while she was gone—and waiting for her to return before he ate.

By the time they finished their dinner, Paige was exhausted, and she knew Cooper had to be every bit as tired as she was. Without a word, he picked up the flashlight and, kit and towel under his arm, made off in the direction of the rest rooms.

Paige cleaned up. She put the food in the ice chest, then got the blankets from the trunk, and made up two pillows. She put Cooper's on the backseat, so he'd have more room. She arranged hers in the front, with Henry on the passenger-side floor. Then she rolled down all the windows, shut the doors, and lay down.

The sound of something striking the trash can outside, accompanied by a sharply bitten-off curse, woke Paige. Quickly she checked to see if Cooper had returned. The backseat was empty.

"Cooper?" she called softly.

Another vivid oath muttered in the dark. Then, "Paige?"

"What are you doing?" she asked, aware of the surrounding campers and darkened campsites.

A large shadow hobbled over to the car. "What am I doing?" Cooper echoed in a low, furious voice. "I'm trying to find the *car,* that's what I'm doing. The batteries in your flashlight died and left me stranded."

"Oh."

"Yeah. Oh." He started around to the passenger side.

"Get in the backseat," Paige instructed him.

He climbed in back. Somehow the seat had seemed much more spacious before, Paige thought. With Cooper lying there now, she could see it was woefully inadequate. It was much too short. He was so tall. The seat was too narrow. Or was it that his shoulders were so wide? At any rate, he didn't look comfortable bunched up like that.

"I thought marines were supposed to be able to find their way around at night," she said, irritated. It wasn't her fault the batteries had died.

"What do I look like? A cat?"

A big one, she thought. A cougar. Tawny. Golden-eyed.

"I mean, aren't you supposed to be able to use the stars?" she persisted.

Cooper thumped the scratchy wool blanket that served as his pillow, trying for a more comfortable shape. "I didn't take my bearings before I left the car because I had a flashlight." He was furious and embarrassed. Couldn't she drop the subject?

As if she'd read his mind, Paige lay back down and silence settled over them.

Cooper brooded.

He was a marine. His father was a marine, and his father before him had been a marine. The tradition of the family's eldest son making his career in the Marine Corps ran back to the Quasi-War with France in the eighteenth century. In all those generations, he wondered, had any of his fighting forebears found themselves in a situation quite this ridiculous?

His father, Colonel Kenneth Sewall Angelsmith—who, thankfully, knew nothing of Cooper's present predicament—had given him a set of toy soldiers when he was five. The colonel had drilled into him the lesson that life was like a battlefield: to gain one's objective, one must know the terrain and deploy available forces to best advantage.

At this moment, the terrain that stretched before Cooper consisted of about twenty-five hundred miles of desert, mountains, and gulf coast. His available forces, Lord help him, had dwindled to a dilapidated car, a hamster, and a crazy woman.

Chapter Three

*S*quee-ak, squee-ak.

Cooper woke instantly.

Squee-ak, squee-ak.

Without moving, he tried to pinpoint the source of the sound.

It was coming from the front seat. The nerve-grating noise wasn't familiar. It could spell danger.

Slowly, with deadly control, Cooper adjusted his position, ready to spring should it be necessary. Inch by slow inch he peered over the back of Paige's seat, every muscle tensed.

There on the front passenger floor, partially illuminated by moonlight, Henry ran in his treadwheel. *Squee-ak, squee-ak*. Metal grated against metal.

Cooper glanced down. Paige was curled up, fast asleep. One hand cushioned her cheek against the roughness of the blanket. The other hand curved into a relaxed, curiously vulnerable cup, resting against her breast, which rose and fell with her even breathing. Her lips were slightly parted. They looked soft. Delectable.

Cooper returned to his hard, narrow bed, twisting and shifting until he found the least uncomfortable position. He closed his eyes, determined to block out the sound of the wheel. Tomorrow would be another horrible day. He'd need his wits about him. Gradually he drifted.

Squee-ak, squee-ak.

Cooper glared into the darkness. Damn rodent. Well, if Paige could sleep through it, he could.

The scraping screech of Henry's wheel continued. Maybe if he could get that miserable rodent to stop running . . .

Using the back of the front seat as a fulcrum, Cooper leaned over. He swiped his arm back and forth, but he couldn't quite reach the cage. Henry paused briefly, then resumed running. That infuriated Cooper. It was as if the hamster had thumbed its nose at him.

Carefully he leaned a little farther forward. He didn't want to wake Paige, though if she could sleep through the racket from the rodent's wheel, probably nothing could wake her.

Cooper's fingertips brushed the bars of the cage. Henry scampered from the wheel to his nest of wood shavings.

"What—? Eeeeeee!"

If Cooper thought that damn wheel was loud, it had nothing on Paige's shriek. Quickly he clamped his hand over her mouth, before she woke all their neighbors. "I was trying to—"

She planted her hands on his chest and shoved, sending him crashing into the back. Before he could get untangled, Paige snatched up the road map.

"How dare you!" She swatted wildly, battering his shoulders, his neck, and his head with frantic, stinging blows.

He raised bent arms to shield his face.

"How could you!" she cried. "I should have *known* you couldn't be trusted. Don't come near me! Don't touch me! You sneaky son of a—" Abruptly she stopped her attack. Paige looked at Cooper, then down at the small cage on the floor. Then back at Cooper. Her eyes narrowed. "You were trying to get to Henry, weren't you?" she said in a soft voice that reminded Cooper of a cobra's warning hiss.

"Yes," he agreed, trying to explain, "he was running in—"

"That does it." She threw open the driver's door and got out.

She jerked open the back door, grabbed Cooper's arm and pulled. He slowly unfolded to perch on the side edge of the seat. She pulled again. He didn't budge.

"Out," she demanded. "I want you out of my car. Now. Anyone who would hurt a harmless little hamster is pond scum and *not* someone I want to travel with."

Lights blinked on in the surrounding campsites. A few campers had come out to investigate the commotion.

Paige tugged on his arm again, but Cooper had reached the limit of his patience. He yanked her into his arms, between his outstretched legs, and settled her on his thigh. "Now," he told her in a low, controlled voice, "if you'll shut up for a minute, I'll tell you what happened."

She struggled to get up. "I will not be intimidated!"

Effortlessly he reseated her. "There's a difference between being intimidated and knowing when to listen. I wasn't trying to hurt your damned hamster."

Her look was skeptical. "Then why were you reaching for him?"

"I wanted to scare him out of that blasted wheel."

"Henry loves that wheel. It's how he gets his exercise."

Cooper found her nearness fractured his concentration. "It, uh, makes enough noise to raise the dead. I don't see how you can sleep through it. I sure can't." The skin of her arms was smooth under his hands. Her straight, silken hair brushed his cheek.

Paige's focus wavered. It was difficult to think of anything but how strong his arms were. Yet they held her gently. A woman could feel safe in such arms. "You'll... you'll get used to it."

Her mouth was a little too wide for conventional beauty, Cooper thought, but he liked it. Her full lips were any man's fantasy. Soft-looking. Tempting. He wondered what they'd feel like, how they'd taste. "I don't want to get used to it. I want to sleep tonight. Take the wheel out of the cage."

He'd helped her with her car from the beginning, Paige admitted to herself. He'd spent three hours working on it this afternoon when it would have been easier, if riskier, to thumb a ride. "The wheel isn't made to be taken out. It will break."

She possessed a crazy kind of courage, Cooper allowed. Stuck in the desert with a broken-down car and little money, she'd coped with things like a trooper. He hadn't seen her cry or heard her whine. "We could lubricate it."

Moonlight gleamed on his high cheekbones, his sensual mouth. Paige thought it made him look dangerous... exciting. In another age he might have been a privateer, running the lines for profit and fancy. In another age she might have been one of his conquests.

But not now.

She straightened. "With what?" she asked briskly. "I don't have any oil."

Cooper noticed the change in her. *She's attracted to me.* He grinned slowly, satisfied.

"What?" she demanded. "What are you smiling about?"

"We have butter," he said, ignoring her question. "We can use that on the wheel."

"Margarine."

"Okay, margarine." He gently brushed her hair behind her ear.

She stared at him, but did not move away.

He gazed at her, and the moment lengthened.

They drifted closer together, as if drawn by an invisible magnet. Cooper tilted his head to kiss her. Paige's eyes fluttered closed.

Squee-ak, squee-ak.

Paige's eyes flew open. *Madness!* She struggled up off Cooper's thigh, out of his hold. For the first time she noticed all the people watching them. "I'll—I'll just get the margarine and put it on the wheel. Good night." She beat a hasty retreat.

Frustrated, Cooper turned and scowled down at Henry, who paused in his nocturnal race. The hamster left his wheel and came to the bars of his cage where he reared onto his plump haunches, his forepaws held up to his breast in a regal hamster pose. His pink nose twitched, as if he didn't like what he smelled. He regarded Cooper with unblinking, unrepentant, beady black eyes.

The challenge had been issued. The war had begun.

Paige woke early the next morning, before the sun fully rose over the mountainous horizon. Stiff and sore, she stretched carefully, hoping to work out some of the kinks. Automobiles were clearly not designed to be slept in overnight, she thought. At least, not this one.

She felt sweaty and grimy and the inside of her mouth tasted like old glue. If she dashed off to the rest rooms now she might beat the crowd and wash in relative privacy.

Cooper still slept, and Paige permitted herself a moment's study of the tall, hard-muscled man. Those piercing eyes were closed now. She could look all she wanted at his mouth with its sensually full top lip, at the contrast between the red gold that shadowed his jaw and the golden brown of his cropped hair.

Quickly she turned away, silently scolding herself for dawdling.

Paige picked up Henry's cage and slipped out of the car. She gathered hamster supplies, her train case, towel, and a change of clothes from the trunk, then hurried up the sandy trail to the rest rooms.

There she changed the cedar shavings in Henry's cage and discovered margarine matted and spiked the hamster's fur. His coat, usually glossy and smooth, was now a greasy mess.

"Oh, poor baby," Paige sympathized as she washed him. "Putting margarine on your wheel was a dumb idea, wasn't it? I'm surprised that man isn't working at the Pentagon."

She was just finishing her own sponge bath when another early riser walked in. Embarrassed, Paige buttoned her blouse, fumbling in her haste.

The other woman, a brunette who looked to be in her late thirties, set her gear down in front of a sink not far from Paige's. "Men," she groaned. "They're worse than kids."

Not knowing what else to do, Paige smiled at her.

"What's with the hamster?"

"It's too hot in the car for him." But not for Cooper. He could bake for all she cared. In fact, she hoped he did. After what he'd pulled last night his comfort wasn't high on her list of priorities.

The woman took a hose and spray attachment out of her nylon duffel bag and slipped the hose end of it over the opening of the faucet. "A *vacation,* I said," the woman continued as she tested the water, then adjusted the flow. "*This* is what we get. Camping. A dinky little tent for our second honeymoon. I *hate* camping," she said emphatically.

Paige pried her gaze away from the sprayer. "So do I." If she had a choice, she'd never spend another night at a campground as long as she lived.

"You want to use this when I'm through?" the brunette offered, indicating the sprayer. "It's the only way you can wash your hair in these places, unless you use the big faucet outside."

Relieved gratitude filled Paige. "Oh, yes, please. That would be wonderful."

"By the way, my name is Shirley Nelson." The woman grinned. "You got shampoo?"

"Yes."

"Good. Then you're all set. This will only take a minute."

They chatted while Shirley washed her hair. Paige agreed whole-heartedly that camping in a tent at Oasis Palms Campground, in the Mojave Desert, in July, was not much of a second honeymoon.

"Where did you want to go?" Paige asked as she turned on the sprayer and bent over the sink. She squeezed a dollop of shampoo onto her wet hair and scrubbed it through.

"Lake Tahoe," Shirley said. "I wanted to see some shows, play the slot machines, and have champagne and strawberries sent up to our room. I wanted to wear something sexy. Ha! Does this look sexy?"

"I can't see."

"Well, wrinkled walking shorts and a sweaty T-shirt are not my idea of sexy." Shirley sighed heavily. "I left Oxnard for this?"

Paige finished rinsing her hair and dried it with her towel. She drained and dried the sprayer and reluctantly returned it to Shirley, thanking her. There wasn't money in the kitty to buy a sprayer. The next time she washed her hair she'd probably end up at an outdoor faucet.

Shirley thrust the sprayer into her duffel. "My pleasure. It's a relief to have someone to talk to, someone I'm not mad at, that is. What are you doing now?"

After combing conditioner through her hair, Paige sectioned off a lock on the top of her head. She reached into her train case and pulled out a pink foam curler. "Doing up my hair. It's naturally straight as a board."

"Wait a minute," the brunette said. "I thought I recognized you. Are you the one who tried to put your guy out of the car last night?"

Paige nearly dropped the curler she was trying to roll into another section of hair. "Uh—"

"Yes! You are, I know you are." Shirley chuckled. "Honey, if that man were mine I'd roll my hair, too. I'd have cosmetic surgery, and liposuction, and anything else it took to keep him, believe me."

She wasn't rolling her hair for Cooper, Paige told herself adamantly. Absolutely not. No, a woman felt better when she knew she looked presentable, that was all. If she was going to be stuck in that hot car with that arrogant marine, she needed every little bit of "feel good" she could get.

"He's not my man," she explained, not wanting Shirley to jump to conclusions about the relationship between Cooper and her. As soon as the words were out she knew she'd have been better off keeping silent.

Shirley's eyebrows rose. "No?" she asked with avid curiosity. "Whose man is he?"

Paige thought furiously. "He's, uh, he's a pretty independent guy," she said. *The man's obnoxious.* She finished rolling the last curl. "He comes and goes as he pleases." *The sooner he's gone, the better. Please let this trip go fast!*

Paige stared into the mirror. A multitude of pink foam-rubber knots studded her scalp. Beauty Woman. She sighed. The arid desert air and hot sun would dry her hair quickly.

"Well, good luck, honey," Shirley said as they walked out of the rest room onto the trail. "With a man like that, you're going to need it."

Paige located the pay phones next to the convenience store. She dialed Maggie, who immediately assured her Waldo was improving.

"He's gettin' better every day. Soon he'll be as ornery as ever. Don't you fret about *him*—he's too cussed to kick off. Those taxes are a bigger worry. Nothin' you can do about it now, though. Just get home as soon as you can." There was a pause, then Maggie said gruffly, "Waldo's asked for you, girl. He frets about you."

Paige's throat tightened at the thought of Waldo, sweet, cantankerous Waldo, laying in an austere hospital room, hooked to machines. She should be there. Waldo needed her.

"I'm on my way, Maggie. I'm just outside Indio, California. I found someone willing to keep the car running in exchange for a ride."

"A stranger?" the old woman asked sharply.

"Not quite." Paige related how she'd met Cooper.

"A marine, eh? There's good and bad in that, dependin' on the man."

"I know."

"Take care, y'hear?"

"I will, Maggie. You, too. I'll call you from Blythe."

She didn't like being so far away from home. Waldo and Paige were Maggie's closest neighbors. The three had come to depend on one another. They were family. Now Maggie was having to drive that ancient pickup truck of hers into Orlando to visit Waldo. Though she wouldn't admit it, driving in city traffic terrified her.

Paige headed back to the campsite. If she didn't get home soon, Maggie might end up in the hospital, too.

After putting everything back in the trunk, Paige spread the towel on the ground next to the car and positioned Henry's cage underneath.

Every cramp, every knot her muscles had acquired from sleeping in the car was amplified when she scrunched up on the towel. Impatience magnified her misery. Finally she dozed.

When she woke, a glance at her watch told her it was 12:20. Cooper would have to get up. They needed to hit the road.

She peered into the open back window to see if he still slept.

Cooper squinted up at her, stopping in the middle of a yawn. His mouth twitched up on one side.

"But soft!" he crooned. "What light through yonder window breaks? It is the east, and Paige is the sun!"

Her curlers. Her face grew so warm she knew it must be the color of a vine-ripened tomato. "Oh, shut up!"

He appeared to study her. "Really," he drawled, "I liked you better with hair."

"You're a real comedian, aren't you? Well, get up, Your Royal Purplety. We need to get on the road. *Some* of us have better things to do than sleep all day."

Pointedly he eyed the curlers. "I can see that."

Without saying another word, she spun on her heel and marched to the rear of the car where she began slapping together sandwiches for breakfast.

She wouldn't take the wretched curlers out until her hair was one hundred percent *dry*. She wanted curls and by heaven she was going to have them. No amount of rudeness from that man was going to stop her!

When he returned clean-shaven from the rest room, dressed in chinos and a white cotton shirt with sleeves rolled up on his forearms, Paige thrust a sandwich at him. She took hers to eat on the opposite side of the car, sitting silently on the towel. She offered a bit of bread to Henry. As she watched him stuff it in his cheek pouch, she stewed.

She hated the effect Cooper had on her. She found it disconcerting, unpredictable. It was just physical, of course. He ranked as a superior specimen of his gender, nothing more. Any healthy, normal woman would feel the twinge. That quiver in her stomach. The increased heart rate. It was irritating.

Paige scowled at an ant laboring across the sand. Emotion didn't begin to enter into her reactions. How could it? Sensitive, considerate men were her type. Not infuriating oafs who made fun of unfortunate women stuck with straight hair. God, the man probably pulled wings off of butterflies, too.

Well, from here on out it would be impersonal all the way. She'd see to that. After last night she knew only too well he'd take advantage of any sign of weakness she showed. He didn't play fair.

Cooper strolled around the car to where Paige sat, and joined her on the towel, brushing against her shoulder. She moved away from him, glaring. "Do you mind?" she demanded.

"I don't if you don't," he said, and took another bite of his sandwich.

"Well, I do. Use your own towel."

"I don't want to get it dirty."

"I see," she said frostily. "But you don't mind getting *mine* dirty."

"You got yours dirty," he pointed out.

He was tricky, too. She'd have to watch that.

"Do the rations permit another sandwich for breakfast?" he inquired with exaggerated civility.

"Yes."

He made another, and bit into it as he walked away from camp, striding in the direction of the convenience store.

"Where are you going?" she called, frustration and curiosity mingling. "We have to leave."

"I'm off to buy you a dozen red roses." He grinned and waved his hand holding the sandwich.

Paige shot to her feet. "I'll leave without you!"

"No you won't." He disappeared from her view behind a camper parked at the site across from theirs.

"Oh, yeah?" Paige breathed. She grabbed up her towel and savagely shook it out, tossing it in the trunk. Quickly she put the food back in the cooler, and retrieved Henry. Then she set Cooper's suitcase neatly on the ground.

She'd show him, Paige fumed. She was tired of putting up with his mule-headed, macho behavior. Push, push, push. Well, this was the end of the line!

Steeped in self-righteousness, Paige slid behind the wheel. She dug in her purse for the keys, but couldn't find them. Seething with frustration, she shook the handbag, but there was no familiar jingle.

Cooper had taken her keys.

* * *

"I loaned you that money three years ago, Rudy. It's time to pay up."

"Yeah, Coop, I know," cajoled the voice on the telephone line. "It's just that I'm a little short of cash right now."

Cooper kept a leash on his temper. He was hot, tired, and his muscles were cramped from having to sleep folded up like a concertina. He didn't want to call in a loan. But the prospect of more campgrounds and sandwiches for every meal made arm-twisting easier.

"You're always a little short of cash, Rudy. I want my money now."

"I don't have it, man."

"Then you'd better borrow it from someone. You should've paid me back years ago."

"Okay, okay. I'm not trying to cheat you out of it."

"Wire it to the Western Union office in Blythe, California."

"Wire it? That costs money, Coop. It's bad enough you're calling collect."

Cooper absently watched a mother with her toddler in hand enter the store. "Be glad I'm not charging you interest, Rudy. I want that money there by four o'clock today, got it?"

"Four o'clock!"

"Can you imagine my reaction if I get to Blythe and discover you haven't wired the money?" Cooper asked in a deceptively pleasant voice.

There was a pause. "I don't want to find out. Okay, Coop. You got your money."

After he hung up, Cooper headed back to the car, tossing the keys up and catching them in his palm. Paige would be ticked at him for taking the keys, but his news should improve her frame of mind. He grinned as he imagined her cautious delight.

Cooper's step slowed. Once they reached Blythe he'd have more than enough money to buy a bus ticket to Jacksonville. He wouldn't need Paige anymore. His fingers tightened involuntarily, and serrated metal bit into flesh. He wouldn't have to put up with that little spitfire or the damned rodent she was so attached to. He could kick back in an air-conditioned coach and leave the driving and worry to someone else.

Without wanting to, he envisioned Paige's face as he told her he was catching a bus home—she was on her own. Her chin would go up fifteen degrees, and the corners of that tender mouth would probably pull down. She'd say something like, "Goodbye, and good riddance. Henry and I can get along just fine without you." And she'd end up stranded on the side of the highway, prey for the first weirdo who came along.

He increased his pace, the behemoth in sight. She wasn't his concern, he told himself angrily. He had his own troubles.

She'd taken her curlers out. It was the first thing he noticed. That wild honey hair of hers rippled down in thick, lustrous waves. But there was something not quite right. It wasn't the fact that the little bully was glaring at him—nothing unusual in that. No, it was something else.

She sat clutching the hamster cage in her lap. "How *dare* you steal my keys!" she cried. "Just who do you think you are?"

Cooper noticed her fingers tremble, and instantly regretted his action, though he couldn't see what other course he could have taken. If he hadn't lifted the keys, she would have driven off without him.

"I couldn't get very far without the car, could I?" he said reasonably.

"It's the principal of the thing," she said, but he could tell her fury was dissolving.

"You would have left without me."

Paige stared down into the cage. Henry turned his back on them, resettling in his nest.

"Isn't that my suitcase there?" The case stood in the sandy campsite like a soloist on stage.

"Yeah." She raised a mutinous gaze to his.

He walked over, picked up the suitcase, and placed it in the trunk of the car. Then he slid into the passenger seat, moving Henry to the floor in back with ostentatious care. He held out the keys to Paige.

She took them, fingering the jagged blades. With a small sigh, she tossed her head, sending honey waves furling back from her cheek.

Cooper knew he was supposed to comment on her hair, to notice the change, like it was a miracle or something. He said the first thing that came to mind.

"I like it better straight."

That was it. That's what was wrong: the difference. He *liked* her hair uncurled. It reminded him of a sheet of silk, a fall of soft rainwater.

Color climbed her cheeks. "Wait a minute while I write that down in my diary," she snapped. "I wouldn't want to forget a gem like that."

"You keep a diary? I'll bet that makes juicy reading."

No, Paige thought. That's why she didn't keep one. Usually her life was pleasantly uneventful. She liked it that way. She'd already had more than her share of turmoil.

Paige knew it was time to discuss something more important than a nonexistent diary with Cooper. She wished she could avoid this conversation, but felt the need to get the matter settled.

"After last night, it's become clear to me we need to set some ground rules for this trip," she stated firmly.

Cooper continued to watch her, but remained silent.

She cleared her throat, and plunged ahead. "I won't put up with any funny business."

"Funny business?"

She met his gaze. "I'm not looking for a good time."

He spread his hands, indicating their view of Oasis Palms Campground. "I think you've achieved your goal admirably."

"You know what I mean," she insisted.

"I'm not sure I do."

Paige narrowed her eyes. Cooper might be obstinate, but he wasn't stupid. He was deliberately baiting her. If bluntness was what he wanted, she'd give it to him.

"I'm not interested in having sex with you, Angelsmith." As soon as the words left her lips, her heart pounded. Sweat moistened her palms.

Cooper's eyes gleamed as he pinned her mercilessly with his gaze. "No?"

She found it hard to breathe. "No."

He bared his teeth in a grin.

Paige forced herself to return his stare unwaveringly. "I'm not into one-night stands—"

"It'll take more than one night to get to Florida."

"—or cheap flings." She inhaled deeply to steady herself for her next words. "Especially with a marine."

His grin vanished. The contours of his face hardened. "What do you have against marines?" he asked in a voice so quiet it sent a chill up her back.

"I grew up a Navy brat, and I saw what my mother went through. I don't want that kind of life—single yet married, the man gone for weeks at a time, sometimes months. And the Marine Corps is as bad about separation as the Navy, maybe worse.''

The smile that curved his mouth was devoid of humor. ''I wasn't proposing.''

Anger licked through Paige, strengthening her. ''No, you weren't, were you? You were propositioning me. Well, I'm not interested in propositions or proposals from you. And if you think I'll trade sex for car repairs, think again, leatherneck.''

He studied her heated face for a moment, then sat back, facing front, in clear dismissal. Casually he slipped his sunglasses back on and folded his arms across his chest.

''Are we understood?'' she persisted, determined to make her point.

''Sure. I'm open to a little fun, and you're not.''

''Just—just keep your distance, Angelsmith.''

''Your wish is my command,'' he drawled.

Eager to get under way, Paige succeeded in starting the car. She headed out of the campground, back to the highway. Next stop, Blythe, California. With luck they'd be well into Arizona by tonight.

''Where did you go with the keys?'' she asked lightly, trying to put the tension behind them.

''I had to make a phone call.'' Cooper continued to gaze out his window.

''And did you?''

He finally looked at her. ''Did I what?''

''Make your phone call.'' She tried to smile.

''Yeah, sugar, I did.'' The line of his mouth hardened. ''When we reach Blythe, I have a surprise for you.''

Chapter Four

Searing air blasted through the open windows as they cruised down Interstate 10. Paige longed to pin the accelerator to the floor and fly over the miles. The speed limit was too *slow*. She released a small, frustrated sigh as she lifted her foot a fraction of an inch and watched the speedometer edge back down to where it was supposed to be.

Her hair whipped around her head, losing, she was certain, every bit of curl she had so carefully induced. In this heat, the alternative—rolling up the windows—was unthinkable. She brushed fine locks from her face, only to have the wind blow them back. She'd pull the darn stuff into a ponytail or a braid when they stopped in Blythe.

She cast a sidelong glance at Cooper. He hadn't spoken since they'd left Indio, an hour ago. His eyes were closed now. For some reason, his sleep made the silence between them more tolerable. She sighed and shifted in her seat, adjusting her sweaty grip on the steering wheel. He was

definitely easier to get along with when he was uncon-
scious.

What was the surprise he planned to spring on her when
they got to Blythe?

Surprises. Paige didn't much care for them. She could
recall only two good surprises in her life. The first was when
Waldo had shown up at her front door, claiming familial
ties. The second was Henry, a gift of love.

She doubted a surprise from Cooper would have anything to do with love.

Was he planning to bail out in Blythe? Paige tried to
swallow, but her throat was too dry. She told herself she'd
be a fool not to expect that. And it wasn't as if he hadn't
already paid for his food and bed. Her chapped lips twisted
in a humorless smile. Actually he'd come off on the short
end of the deal. Sandwiches and the backseat of an old car.

There was a small catch in her in-drawn breath as she
thought about another breakdown, this time with no help.
She tried for a brighter outlook. Maybe... maybe the car
would hold together until she made it back to Plymouth. If
she watched her speedometer, and carried plenty of water...

If pigs could fly.

What other possibilities were there? She could hitchhike. Immediately her mind forced aside that idea. No, she
couldn't. Not after what had happened to Emily Pearson.
Even though the incident had taken place back in her senior year of high school, Paige remembered it with terrible
clarity. Emily had hitched a ride from St. Augustine....

Paige knew she'd just have to drive and hope for the best.
She expected the worst.

No, she didn't like surprises.

Cooper stirred and stretched as best he could in the space available. "Amazing," he mumbled. "The thing's still running."

Paige said nothing.

"Any sign of car trouble?" he asked, rubbing his eyes. "No."

He glanced first at the dials, gauges, and lights on the dashboard, then at Paige's closed face, trying to read both.

What was wrong with her? She'd been so cheerful when they'd left the campground, and now he woke up to monosyllables.

"Did I snore?" he asked, impatient with her mood.

"I didn't notice."

Yeah. Right.

"Well, what *did* you notice? The speedometer? Did you notice you're going over fifty-five? Didn't we agree not to go over fifty-five miles an hour?" Fifty-five crawling miles an hour. It would take *years* to get across country.

She snapped a horrified gaze down to the speedometer. Immediately he saw the red line swing down.

"I lost track," she muttered.

His impatience escalated into irritation. "Losing track like that will overheat the car. I don't know about you, but I don't enjoy sitting on the side of the road. I've got places to go, things to do."

Paige gripped the wheel tighter. "I'll remember that."

When he spoke, the words were deceptively mild. "See that you do."

She glared at him. Her mouth tightened, but she remained silent.

Something was wrong here, but Cooper couldn't figure it out since Paige refused to talk. He tried another angle.

"How long since we left Indio?" He couldn't remember them getting on the interstate. He must have dropped off like a rock.

"A little over an hour."

He looked at the map and calculated they should be rolling into Blythe in about another hour. If Rudy had wired the money, Cooper would have a decent meal and a shower tonight. The thought brought such bliss it embarrassed him. In his profession, it was foolish to form too great an attachment to creature comforts.

He settled into the corner of his seat and closed his eyes again. Asleep, he couldn't worry about what Nathan might have done to their business. The business Cooper had created and nurtured. Asleep, he couldn't remember what it was like to hold Paige in his arms and have her gaze at him with that soft, faintly startled, woman look.

He sighed and crossed his arms over his chest, willing his mind clear of troubles.

"What surprise?" Paige demanded abruptly.

Cooper blinked.

She turned her eyes from the road to meet his. "I want to know about this little bombshell. I haven't had much luck with such things in the past. Don't you think you at least owe me a little honesty?"

So that was it. He had worried her with his announcement. It hadn't been his intention, but now he could see how she might be concerned.

"You mean like when you told me you'd 'finance' our trip?" he asked. "I owe you very little honesty, I'd say."

The color drained from her cheeks and he could have kicked himself. When she didn't reply, he felt even worse. "Well?" he prompted, wanting a response, any response.

"You're going to leave, aren't you?" she said in a low voice that reached into him and wrung something in his chest. She stared at the highway ahead.

He didn't move from his corner. "Paige, I told you I'd stay with you to Plymouth," he said softly. "I gave my word as an officer and a gentleman."

Paige turned and searched his face, afraid of what she'd find. Eyes the color of Renaissance gold gazed back at her.

Was there a corner on this earth where such vows still held meaning? Were there still those who maintained such a romantic ideal as honor?

They didn't talk the rest of the way to Blythe. There, they stopped at a filling station. Cooper pumped gas while Paige went inside to pay for their fuel and ask directions.

They arrived at the Western Union office to find the money had arrived.

Paige received the news with mixed feelings of dread and elation. Elation they might make it home, dread that Cooper would catch more reliable transportation east. If he stayed with her, she silently vowed to repay him every cent spent on her behalf.

"Come on," he said, directing her out the door. "We're going to a bank to get traveler's checks. Can't afford to take any chances with this money."

She wanted to know how much had been wired, but couldn't bring herself to ask. It wasn't her money.

He grinned, exuberant. "First stop after the bank is the bus station for two one-way tickets east. An air-conditioned straight shot. No more stopping by the side of the road to humor a decrepit radiator."

Bus? He was going to buy her a bus ticket? Greyhound would get her to Waldo and to the Orange County tax collector quickly and comfortably.

Her throat threatened to close all the way. "I can't," she choked.

He stopped abruptly. "Can't? What do you mean you *can't?* I'm going to pay for it. There's enough money here for motel rooms tonight, a good meal, and two—count them—*two* bus tickets."

"Honest, it's not me. I *want* to take the bus. And I appreciate your offer. But the bus company won't let me take Henry. I can't...." Her throat did close. After two breaths she tried again. "I can't leave without Henry." God, Cooper was going to leave her behind and she couldn't even blame him.

"You can get another hamster when you get to Florida. You said yourself it's old. The thing might not even make it all the way to Plymouth."

She didn't say anything. She couldn't. She just stood there, miserable, staring down at the top of Henry's cage, trying not to think beyond the moment.

Cooper swore. He rounded and stormed away from her several paces.

After a moment, Paige ventured a glance up.

He stood with his back to her, one hand anchored in his hair.

"This is crazy," he growled. "Pure, stupid craziness!"

His tone told her he was trying to understand. She held her breath.

"And all over a damned hamster. A glorified *rat!*" He swung around and marched back to her. Cooper stabbed a finger toward the cage she clutched to her middle. "All I can say is, that rodent better not die on us before we get to Plymouth!" And with that he stalked to the car.

Paige stared blankly after him. He wasn't going to take the bus. He was turning down dependable, fast, *air-conditioned* transportation to stay with her.

Why?

Quickly she scrambled after him. Now wasn't the time to ask.

As they left the bank, Cooper handed Paige seven hundred dollars in small denomination traveler's checks. She looked up at him.

When he saw her expression, Cooper knew he'd done the right thing. He saw a bus sweep down the interstate in the distance, and thought maybe he hadn't done the *smart* thing, but he could live with that.

She hesitated, then tried to give the checks back to him.

"No," he said firmly, clasping his hands around hers, closing her fingers over the crisp paper. "From the start, you've been the treasurer of this little jaunt. I see no reason to change that. There's seven hundred dollars here. I think we can afford an inexpensive room, and some cooked meals. The rest goes to gas and parts for the car."

Paige looked down at their hands. He wasn't going to leave. Cooper was going to honor his promise. Suddenly she felt like crying. Relief, trembling and weakening, flooded through her. Stubborn pride kept her from throwing her arms around his neck and dampening the front of his shirt with grateful tears. Yet she knew he deserved her thanks.

She raised her eyes to his. "Cooper, I—" Something he'd said struck her. "*A* room? *One* room?"

A slow smile moved across his face.

"Both of us? Together? In one room?" Warning signs flashed in her brain.

He shrugged. "You're in charge of the money. It's up to you. If you feel certain we won't need much for car repairs, then, by all means, we'll get two rooms."

Quickly she made some mental calculations. Then, still clutching the traveler's checks, she disengaged her hands from his.

She hated it when he was right.

"One room," she agreed grudgingly.

He ushered her back to the car and slid into the driver's seat. Paige set Henry in the backseat and dropped the keys into Cooper's waiting palm. She wanted to wipe that smile off his face. It was altogether too satisfied. Too knowing.

On the other side of Blythe, just out of town, the car overheated. Cooper frowned at the red idiot light. Without a word, he pulled over and got out. Carefully he raised the hood. White steam escaped.

Paige climbed out of the car and came to stand next to Cooper. The old radiator clicked and popped as the water boiled inside.

She stated the obvious, just to break the silence. "It's the radiator again."

He huffed out a sharp breath. "No fooling *you*," he said disgustedly.

"Why did it overheat? We were going fifty-five."

Cooper plowed widespread fingers through short hair. "It's hot out. We've been driving for a few hours. We've been turning the engine on and off, never leaving it off long enough to cool down. Hell, I don't know," he ended impatiently, frustrated. "Maybe it just hates us."

At Paige's silent reprimand, he sighed. "Maybe there's more damage than I saw."

Her heart sank. "Which means...?"

"We'll have to slow down even more. Try fifty instead of fifty-five."

At this rate she'd never get home. Paige groaned.

Cooper gave her a crooked smile. "My sentiments exactly."

While they waited for the engine to cool, Paige sat in the open car, on the edge of the passenger seat, with the hamster cage on her lap. She fanned a panting Henry with the road map. "Oh, I know," she crooned softly. "The desert isn't a good place for hamsters. It's too hot and dry. But tonight you'll get to sleep in a motel room. Just think, Henry. Air-conditioning. Won't that be nice?" Even as she spoke, Paige imagined how it would feel to have cool air slipping over her skin like satin. A respite from hell.

She couldn't see any improvement in Henry, so she fanned the map more vigorously. "Please hang in there, little man," she pleaded.

"Ready to roll?" Cooper asked as he twisted the cap back on the plastic water jug, after filling the radiator.

Paige placed Henry in back, then quickly took her seat on the passenger side. Under Cooper's coaxing, the behemoth lumbered back out onto the highway, headed toward Arizona.

Paige tried to settle into her corner, but discovered she couldn't sleep. Instead her eyes were drawn to Cooper. From under lowered lashes she felt free to observe him. The way the wind stroked through his tawny hair, tousling the longer, wavy top. The gleam of the sun on his broad, high cheekbones. Long, curved eyelashes struck her as being incongruous, curiously vulnerable, in a face that was otherwise so unconditionally masculine. The lids of his cougar eyes were wide and sensual, giving him the appearance of a man used to having his way with women, a man who knew the whys and wherefores of good, satisfying sex. Paige swallowed dryly. His mouth, sculpted into a promise of pleasure, only confirmed that impression.

Cooper's shoulders were his most telling feature. They were wide, hard, and stubborn. In Paige's mind they echoed his character: hard and stubborn. Yet...they supported much of her burdens as well as his own.

She shifted, seeking a little comfort. In her life she needed many things, she told herself, but not a marine. Never a marine. Damn, Paige thought irritably, would this heat never let up?

From the slow deepening of her breathing, Cooper knew when Paige finally drifted into sleep. He'd been aware of being surveyed. The feel of her gaze moving over him had made his body tighten.

He glanced over at her. Dark blond lashes created sweet crescents. Pale brown freckles scattered across the bridge of her nose and the top of her cheeks. Cooper was tempted to press a kiss to her slightly parted lips, slipping his tongue between them, tasting her.

He frowned at the highway and purposefully thought of Nathan and of Cooper's Classics, unleashing a rush of anger and concern.

The Arizona inspection station was in sight, just within the state border, when Paige woke. She stared sleepily at it for a moment, her sluggish brain attaching some significance to the building and its function. Like a pebble into a pond, realization plunked into awareness, sending out eddies of alarm.

With a squawk, Paige whipped around to snatch up Henry's cage from the back. Quickly she dumped the contents of her purse into an empty paper sack that had contained the last of the apples they'd bought in Indio.

"What are you doing?" Cooper asked, his attention divided between the line of cars awaiting passage through the station and Paige's activity.

She groped under the driver's seat, causing Cooper to shift his legs out of her way. "We're coming to the state inspection station," she said, her words muffled. She found what she needed: a roll of plastic wrap.

"I can see that. Maybe I should ask *why* you're doing this."

She lined her tote with the plastic, followed by a layer of paper towels. Then she opened the cage and gently withdrew Henry. Carefully she deposited him in her spacious handbag, and partially closed the top, allowing for air. Opening her door a crack, she dumped the wood shavings onto the highway.

"Paige." Cooper's word was a sharp command.

She smoothly collapsed the cage and slid it under her seat, then settled back to wait. "This is a border inspection station, right? They check for things they don't want coming into their state: plants, drugs—"

"Rodents."

"—animals," she ended flatly.

Cooper watched the border guards make a cursory inspection of the car ahead of them. "I doubt they'd refuse entry to a pet hamster."

The thought of them taking Henry from her made her fingers tighten on the top of her purse. "I can't take that chance."

"What if they search your purse?"

Her stomach twisted. "They didn't last time."

"You mean on the trip out?"

She nodded, refusing to take her eyes from the inspector. Her breath caught in her throat when the man turned and motioned them forward.

As with the car in front of them, the official was courteous and the inspection brief. Paige released a deep, thankful sigh when they were allowed to pass. As soon as they were a safe distance away from the station, she carefully lifted Henry from her purse.

She knew he wasn't happy. His nose twitched furiously as he stared at her with reproachful black eyes.

"Pull over," she told Cooper.

He gave her a questioning look, but complied.

"Here." With one hand she arranged Cooper's hands into a cup. Before he could protest, she placed Henry into it. "Be careful with him."

"Hey!" He glared first at Paige, then at the disgruntled ball of brown and white fur he held. "I don't handle rats."

Henry quivered, as if in indignation.

Paige swiftly reassembled the travel cage, and filled it with wood shavings. "Henry is *not* a rat. And he's very sensitive, so I'd advise you not to insult him." She hooked his filled water bottle in place.

"What the—" Cooper stared down at the hamster with widening eyes. "Damn it! I'm going to—"

In one rapid motion, Paige removed Henry from danger, scooping him out of Cooper's soiled hands. She settled him tenderly in fragrant shavings. "There you are, baby," she lilted, stroking his ruffled fur. She set the cage in back, out of easy reach from the driver. Trying hard not to laugh, she turned to face an outraged Cooper.

"Filthy little beast!" he raged as she washed his hands with pre-moistened towelettes. "Disgusting!"

"Henry was nervous," she reasoned, struggling against a smile.

"Like hell! That beady-eyed little rodent hates me." He regarded Henry narrowly. "He's hated me from the first."

"You haven't been very nice to him, either."

Cooper swung his head around to fix her with an indignant look.

"Well you haven't," she insisted, dropping the towelettes into a litter bag.

"Oh, I see. It's all my fault. I guess I should be grateful you don't have a pet elephant."

She realized she was still holding Cooper's hand. It was larger than hers and well made, with long, blunt-tipped fingers. For an instant she was tempted to measure her palm against his, to touch him when there really was no direct need. No need but her own.

Instead she released him.

He brought his lemon-scented hands up to cup her face, moving closer until she could feel his breath tease her lips. His eyes searched her face.

He was going to kiss her, Paige told herself as tiny stars of anticipation shot through her. He was going to lower his mouth over hers and finally kiss her.

Cooper stared at her mouth. Soft. Lush. When her lips parted, desire knifed through him so sharply he teetered on the edge of pain.

He wanted Paige. Badly. But his wanting was tangled with other, unexpected responses. Responses that made him uneasy because he couldn't put a finger on them.

He was most comfortable with women who could take care of themselves. He'd been raised in a way of life where women were continually called upon to draw on inner strength. As a man, he expected it. Strong women were survivors.

He was unsure of Paige's strength. He sensed it was defensive, like armor. And, like armor, worn to protect something vulnerable inside. She called forth in him a protectiveness unfamiliar in its intimacy. It touched him and left him vaguely confused.

Slowly he lowered his hands, easing back, away from her. Cars and trucks passed on the highway, lashing bursts of hot wind into the car through its open windows.

He wished he couldn't see the surprise in her eyes. It
made him feel inadequate. The shuttered look that
promptly followed excluded Cooper from her feelings,
shaming him.

She had effectively withdrawn any rights he might possibly have earned. As he started the engine and brought the
car back onto the highway, he suddenly felt bereft and more
alone than he'd felt in many solitary years.

Paige couldn't understand why Cooper had drawn back.
He'd wanted to kiss her, of that she was certain. Then he'd
changed his mind. She burned with humiliation. How could
she have been so stupid as to have actually *wanted* Cooper's kiss? Stupid? Weak was more like it. Stupidly weak.
She sat well on her side of the car, staring woodenly ahead.
The knowledge that she *did* want him to kiss her, to hold
her, stuck like a thorn in her pride. Well, she'd just have to
exercise some self-control, that was all.

For almost an hour the only sounds in the car were those
of the engine, the wind, and the interstate traffic. Paige
staunchly told herself she liked it that way, but she knew a
lie when she heard one.

Abruptly Cooper asked, "Why are you so attached to
that hamster? I mean, I could understand it if you felt that
way about a dog, or a cat. But a hamster?" His tone was
casual, as if there had never been an unpleasant moment
between them.

A stranger asking another stranger a personal question,
Paige thought sourly. Grudgingly she decided to help him
keep the peace. "My father was in the Navy. We moved
around a lot, and some of the places we went required a
long quarantine for animals. My mother felt a husband, a
child and a household were enough to cope with." She
shrugged, remembering how badly she had wanted a
brother or sister, then, failing that, a dog or a cat. *Some-*

one to call her own. A friend and confidant she wouldn't
have to leave behind each time her father received new orders. "Henry is the first pet I've ever had," she told Cooper. "Waldo gave him to me."

Waldo believed in the warmth of friendship, believed it
wasn't limited to two-legged animals. And Waldo believed
Paige had been alone entirely too much of her life. She
smiled fondly. The day her cousin had appeared at her front
door had been the luckiest day of her life.

And now he was isolated in a hospital room. He needed
her, and she wasn't there. Tears rose up to burn Paige's
eyes. With a will, she kept them at bay. She turned her
head, pretending to look out the side window.

"Who's Waldo?" Cooper asked, pulling out to pass an
eighteen-wheeler.

"A friend. A relative." She was pleased her voice
sounded normal.

"Relative?" He glanced at her, then back at the road.

If she hadn't known better she might have almost believed he was really interested. "Cousin." Distant cousin by
birth rank. Ranked by heart, he was her grandfather and
best friend.

"Do you have a big family?"

"No. Do you?"

"Just the usual. Mother, father... brother."

"A brother." Paige smiled at Cooper. "I always wanted
a brother."

"You can have mine."

His offer was so tart, Paige laughed. "Gee, I don't know.
Maybe brothers aren't the treasures I thought they were."

"Depends on the brother, I imagine."

She tried to read his expression. "And I'll bet you were
perfect," she teased. "Never tattled. Always shared your

toy trucks. Stuck up for your brother when the chips were down.''

Cooper didn't respond for a moment, and Paige wondered if she'd offended him.

"No one's perfect," he said at last, sounding thoughtful.

He seemed disinclined to continue the conversation. Reluctant to intrude on his silence, Paige leaned back into the seat and watched the desert roll by.

Two and a half hours later, Cooper stopped the car on the shoulder and reached for the battered road map. He spread it out over the steering wheel and studied it.

"Are we lost?" Paige asked.

Slowly he shook his head, concentrating on the map. "No." He looked over at her and pointed to a place on the map.

Paige scooted toward him, from the far side of the seat, to see what he was pointing at. His fingertip pinned the paper close to Phoenix.

"City traffic would be hard on the car. If we turn off here," he indicated a road connecting with the highway, "we can avoid Phoenix altogether."

"Will it take longer?" she asked anxiously.

Again Cooper pointed to the map, tracing the detour for her to see. "It shouldn't take much longer, and it'll save wear and tear on the car."

His suggestion sounded reasonable, but Paige would have felt better taking the more populated route. The detour looked as if it would take them through desolate territory.

Reluctantly she agreed.

Cooper folded the map and handed it to Paige to put in the glove compartment. He started the car and merged with the highway traffic. "Are you hungry? What about lunch?"

The ice chest was in the backseat, with Henry. Paige thought about recommending they stop long enough for sandwiches and lemonade. They could eat without rushing wind, road vibration or the constant thrum of the engine, and when they were finished, she could take her turn behind the wheel. Only the urgent nature of their journey kept her quiet.

Raising up on her knees, her back to the dashboard, she reached over the seat and opened the cooler. It wasn't easy making sandwiches from that position, but she finally managed. They'd have to forego the lemonade she'd made. The ice chest was full so she'd packed the drink container in the trunk. The thought of eating another sandwich, without even something to drink, was unappealing.

Cooper bit off a blistering oath and steered to the side of the road. He turned off the ignition.

Paige's eyes flew to the instruments on the dash. The engine light shone clear, brilliant red.

Chapter Five

Cooper folded his arms on the steering wheel and dropped his forehead onto them. "Oh, hell," he muttered.

He looked so frustrated, so disconsolate, Paige refrained from pointing out that, thanks to him, they were now in the middle of nowhere. She handed him his sandwich.

Looking up, he stared blankly at the offering, then took it, smiling faintly. "Thanks." Instead of taking a bite, he got out of the car. He left his door open, and opened the one in back, as well, to help keep the temperature down inside the car. Paige followed suit, then checked on Henry.

Sandwich gripped between his teeth, Cooper wrapped a rag around his hand and opened the hood. Water bubbled and hissed inside the radiator.

Paige came to stand next to him, filled with discouragement. "Do we go forty-five miles an hour from now on?"

Cooper removed his sandwich from the grip of his jaws, chewing a bite. He swallowed. "Looks like it."

She wanted to cry. The radiator just kept getting worse. The next time it overheated they might be truly stranded in this arid land.

She felt a soft nudge against her arm, and looked up at Cooper in question.

He met her gaze with a crooked smile. "Chin up, sugar. We aren't licked yet. I thought this radiator could be coddled into getting us east, but there might be too much damage. If so, we'll find a junkyard and get another one." He gave her an awkward pat on her shoulder. "Trust me, we'll make it through this."

Paige squinted up at him. "Do you really believe that?" She needed honesty.

"Affirmative."

She worried her bottom lip between her teeth, thinking maybe now wasn't a good time to break the news. On the other hand, it might be wise to take advantage of his positive frame of mind.

"Even if you knew we'd picked up a nail in the right rear tire?" she asked.

"What?"

She hated being the bearer of bad news. "I said—"

"Damn it, I know what you said!" Savagely he bit another piece from his sandwich, then thrust the remaining portion into Paige's fingers. "Put that somewhere safe. I'll eat it later."

He stripped off his shirt and slung it onto the front seat. Then he stamped around to the trunk and began clearing everything out to get to the lug wrench, spare tire and jack. Paige deposited his sandwich in the ice chest, then rushed to help him. Before they reached what he needed, suitcases, half a dozen plastic jugs of water and lemonade, and a toolbox had been transferred to the hot asphalt.

Cooper jacked up the car, then fit the tip of the wrench to a lug nut on the wheel and tried to turn it. The large nut remained unmoved. He twisted again, applying more pressure.

Paige stared at him as he worked, mesmerized by the sight of muscle rippling under gleaming skin. So much muscle, bunching into granite, elongating into steel cord, under so much sun-browned, smooth skin.

He tried to loosen the nut a third time, straining against the wrench. Sinews ridged his neck, arms, shoulders and back. After a minute he expelled his pent breath in a deep-throated grunt and let up.

Paige found one of the jugs of lemonade and poured them each a glass. She added ice from the bag in the cooler, and brought Cooper his drink. He took it from her with a nod of appreciation.

He could have taken a bus, she reminded herself. By now he'd have been well on his way to the New Mexico state border. Instead here he was, working on her broken-down car in the blazing desert heat. She wasn't sure she believed a man's honor could be carried so far, but whatever his reason, he deserved more courtesy, more patience than he'd had from her so far. True, it was hot and she was worried, but Paige knew Cooper was hot, too, and, she suspected, very worried about something in Jacksonville.

She smiled as she took the empty glass from him. "More?"

For an instant his eyes betrayed his astonishment, and she vowed to be nicer to him for the rest of the trip.

"Please," he said.

Paige hummed as she went about fixing him more iced lemonade. Yes, being congenial would make the trip so much easier.

After Cooper accepted the drink and swallowed a few gulps, he set it aside, ready to get back to work. "These nuts are stuck. I need your help."

"All right," she agreed, uncertain of what he expected of her.

He indicated the wrench still attached to the lug nut. "Stand on this and bounce up and down." As if it was the most natural thing in the world, he took her hand and assisted her up onto the narrow parallel bar of the wrench.

Paige found she liked the way his warm fingers and palm gently enclosed hers. There was strength in his hold, yet care given not to overwhelm. Without thinking, she looked into his amber eyes. What she saw there caused her to nearly lose her footing.

Desire. Desire and something...else. Something she couldn't quite read. Something that overpowered even the raw wanting she found in his gaze, and made her feel physically safe, but emotionally endangered.

Cooper looked away first, ducking his head. He released her hand, leaning down to steady the wrench. Paige was left with only his slick back to steady herself. She could feel his iron muscles move as he shifted his stance.

"Bounce," he instructed.

"Uh, right." Gingerly she sought her balance on her precarious perch, preparing herself.

"You call that a bounce?" Cooper asked.

"I haven't done anything yet." Her hand slipped, and she wobbled.

Cooper peered up at her from over his lowered shoulder. "Grab onto my belt."

Reluctantly, Paige hooked her fingers between the fabric of his trousers and his leather belt. "Okay," she announced. "I'm going to bounce."

She gave a careful hop.

"Try again." Cooper glanced up from his bent position.

Paige hopped again. "How's that?"

Cooper hadn't failed to notice the alluring sway of Paige's breasts. "Jump harder."

She took a deep breath. "Here goes." Gripping his belt tightly, she hopped up and down in rapid succession.

It was a sight to stir a man's fantasies. At that instant Cooper forgot the flat tire. He forgot the lug nut. He forgot everything but beautifully bouncing Paige.

"Is it loose?"

"Huh?" *Loose?* Was she kidding?

She looked at him expectantly. "Is it coming?"

He could tell she was wearing a bra, but she filled it with one hundred percent all-American female. Cooper liked that in a woman.

"Should I bounce some more?" The exasperation in her voice caught his attention.

Quickly he checked the nut. It had turned, though barely.

"Yeah," he told her. "Bounce some more."

This time Paige's antics did the job. Regretfully he helped her down from the wrench.

God was merciful. There were three other resistant lug nuts.

By the last one, Paige was battling a scowl. She felt like an idiot, hopping up and down like a demented kangaroo. If only she could be more like Cooper, she thought ruefully. He didn't complain about the heat or the work. In fact, the man was downright cheerful.

"That should do it," he said, and straightened to assist her back to earth.

He paused, facing her, and for a few seconds she thought he wanted to say something. Sunlight glinted off his gleaming body.

The moment passed as Cooper gave her a fleeting half smile, then went back to changing the tire.

Paige sat down next to Henry's cage. Absently she picked up the map and fanned him.

She didn't want to like that man. Not Cooper. Not stubborn, sarcastic, dependable, irresistible Cooper.

As much as she wanted to, Paige's honesty wouldn't allow her to believe she rejected *him*. It was what she felt for him. Physical attraction. Sharp and heady, it crackled between them like an electrical charge. And something else had grown with it. Something inexplicable.

No, she didn't want to like Cooper.

But she did.

And he was a marine.

Paige didn't want a marine. Or a sailor, or a soldier. She wanted a civilian.

But Cooper was, basically, a good man. She decided there could be no harm in liking him. Liking him was okay. She just couldn't love him. Paige almost laughed as she walked to the trunk and began reloading suitcases. Love him? There was absolutely, positively no chance of *that*. A bigger worry was their mutual case of lust.

"Paige, bring me one of the jugs of water," Cooper called from the front of the car.

Startled, she banged her head on the inside of the trunk lid, biting off an oath. She rubbed the sore spot as she peered around to the front of the car.

Hands propped on slim hips, Cooper regarded the radiator. He'd made a headband out of a handkerchief, and his ruffled golden brown hair waved over the top of it. He leaned forward, reaching for something under the hood, out of her line of sight. All she could see were splendidly developed muscles working over a perfectly tapered torso. Chinos pulled taut across the hard curve of male buttocks.

Her mouth went dry.

"Paige!" Cooper's voice trumpeted impatience.

Hastily she snatched up one of the dozen jugs and hurried to hand it to him.

"Thanks." He twisted the cap off the jug and poured the contents into the radiator. "Everything loaded?"

"All set."

"Good. We can—" He stopped, frowning slightly as if puzzled.

He sniffed the air over the radiator. His frown deepened as he raised the open mouth of the empty jug to his nose and sniffed again.

The tendons in his hands and wrists jumped as he crushed the gallon container.

Paige's eyes grew large and, despite herself, she backed up a step. "What's wrong?"

"You gave me lemonade," he said in a deathly quiet voice. "Now it's in the radiator, sugar and all."

His words struck a blow to her stomach. She stared at the now-empty jug in horror. Lemonade!

Cooper turned on his heel. Circling the far side of the car from Paige, he strode to the trunk. He hurled down the empty container and picked up a full one, pulled off the cap and inhaled. He followed the same procedure with a second and a third.

"Bring me all the water," he ordered in a controlled voice when Paige remained immobilized. "*Just* the water."

Paige was so furious with herself she wanted to scream. Furious and mortified. She walked to the rear of the car and inspected the remaining bottles.

Cooper flushed out the radiator in stony silence.

Paige fanned Henry.

"Too bad you can't fix cars," she muttered to the hamster. She watched as Cooper dropped the hood into place. "We'd all be happier." Especially Cooper.

He'd have been ensconced in a temperature-controlled bus with no cares about tires or radiators. Or lemonade. Instead, poor man, he was stuck here, hot and sweaty.

An idea struck. Paige dropped the map on the seat and hurried to the trunk. She soaked a rag from the only jug of water left.

She couldn't put Cooper on the bus, but she could make certain he wasn't sweaty.

"Hold still a minute," she commanded softly as he started to get into the car. She smiled when he cast a suspicious look at her.

Paige lifted his headband off and carefully drew the wet cloth across his forehead. When he didn't stop her, she gained the courage to stroke the high, wide planes of his cheeks, one at a time.

Cooper closed his eyes, and she moved the cool, wet cloth over his eyelids. Then his nose. Then his chin. When he didn't stir, she lightly brushed his lips. His was a mouth that could be both commanding and sexy. A mouth that had come close to kissing her.

She swabbed his neck and was surprised when he tilted his head back, exposing his throat. She obliged him. He moaned deeply, a sound of profound pleasure. Hearing it sent tiny shock waves through Paige. She found she wanted to stand on her toes and press her lips to the juncture of his throat and shoulder. Instead she touched it with the damp cloth. His deep chest with its thatch of brown hair was too intimidating. Disconcertingly masculine, it implied a power that sent her hand skimming nervously to his back.

High along each shoulder, he had a dusting of freckles, evidence of at least one sunburn. She found it difficult to breathe as she envisioned Cooper stretched out on the beach, worshipping the sun.

She stroked his back slowly, leaving a wet trail for the desert air to dry. The temptation to rest her cheek against that broad expanse was strong. Maybe she could hear his heartbeat. Maybe it was as rapid as hers.

When she glided the cloth down the long center indentation and neared his waist, he reached back and grasped her wrist.

Cooper told himself she didn't realize the effect her actions had on him. The powerful tightening, the urgent demand. He turned to face her and took the cloth from her hand. "Get in the car," he told her shortly.

She must have understood then, because color rose in her face, and she quickly moved around to the driver's seat.

He rubbed down his chest and arms with the rag, then carefully settled into the passenger side of the seat.

He could feel her gaze on him and, to his irritation, the warmth of a flush crept up his neck.

She cleared her throat. "Cooper, I—I didn't... What I mean to say is..." Her words trailed off, as if she realized what she meant to say would only embarrass them both.

Cooper attempted a reassuring smile. "It was a nice thought. I feel...cleaner...now."

And hotter than ever. Where Paige Ruegger was concerned, his brain and body seemed to have a parting of the ways. He picked up his shirt and pulled it back on, buttoning all the buttons.

Mariachi music filled the car. That and Mexican commentary, which Cooper couldn't understand, were the only things the radio would pick up. For the first hour it had been cheerful. Now it was getting on his nerves.

Paige watched the road ahead, occupied by her own thoughts, which left Cooper to review for the hundredth time the situation with his credit, his brother, and his business.

What had happened to all of them? At his brother's number he received the recorded message of the answering machine. When he dialed Cooper's Classics no one answered.

Where was Nathan? Was he ill? In some kind of trouble? Why wasn't someone answering the telephone at Classics?

Cooper hated the feeling of powerlessness that came with his inability to reach Nathan, to find out what was going on.

He should have taken the bus. He should have left Paige with her damned precious pet and taken the bus. He could have ordered her to stay in Blythe until he wired her money from Jacksonville. But he knew she wouldn't listen. She was in a rush to get to Plymouth. Something there demanded her immediate attention. Something important to her.

Cooper considered the predicament with self-deprecating disgust. The little spitfire wasn't his responsibility. Life was full of choices, and if she chose to keep the rodent with her instead of boarding a bus home, well, that was her choice. No skin off his nose. Why should he care?

But he did. Just the thought of her being stranded on the side of the road knotted his stomach. A marooned woman who looked as good as Paige would attract all kinds of predators. Cooper told himself he couldn't live with that on his conscience.

He turned his thoughts in a more constructive direction: the radiator. Trying to replace it was a bad idea. The tool set Stan Butterworth had loaned him was complete enough to make smaller, more basic car repairs, but the set couldn't handle the tearing out and installing of something as involved as a radiator.

He'd need a place to work. Time was also a consideration. They'd be lucky if the job only took one full day.

And then there was the cost. He estimated a decent radiator for this model car would run about a hundred dollars. They'd also have to buy hoses to replace the ones that would probably crumble in his hands when he tried to remove them.

Before he replaced the radiator, Cooper decided, it needed to get a lot worse than it was now.

Just after nine o'clock, they stopped for the night. Paige stayed with the car while Cooper went in to register.

Only minutes before, she had been exhausted and sleepy. But now, watching the buzzing neon sign blink Motel, Motel, Motel, she was starkly awake.

She reached for Henry's cage, setting it on her lap. He paused in his wheel, staring up at her with bright black eyes. His nose twitched as if he tried to detect her trouble.

"Try and be a little quieter tonight," she told him. "We don't want to keep Cooper awake, do we? It's important he get a full night's sleep. All night." She hoped Cooper would fall asleep immediately and not wake up until it was time to leave in the morning. She hoped she could, too.

Cooper returned with a key and drove them around to the far side of the motel where they unloaded their suitcases, the ice chest, and Henry.

Cooper closed and locked the door behind them as they came in for the night. The moment Paige had been dreading since Blythe had arrived.

Suitcase in hand, she surveyed the tiny room. Most of it was taken up by the two double beds.

Wall-to-wall bed. Not an arrangement conducive to maintaining distance from a sexy man who'd already informed her he was open to fun and games.

"You can put your suitcase down now." His grin told her he'd guessed what she was thinking.

She heaved it onto the low bureau and fumbled with the clasps.

Cooper moved in her direction, but stopped. "Ladies first," he said, gesturing toward the bathroom.

"Uh, thanks." Paige grabbed her robe, nightgown, and train case and hastened to accept his offer.

The sound of the door closing brought Cooper a fragment of relief. Spending the night in the same room with Paige, with so much available bed, was going to be harder than he'd thought. He'd be able to enjoy the air-conditioning a lot more if he wasn't so agitated.

He heard the shower come on.

An image sprang into his mind.

Water sluicing over Paige's upturned face, over her arched throat, over pert breasts. Her nipples would be erect and ready to be rolled between a man's thumb and finger. They'd be pink, because she was blond. And if she was a real blond...

Cooper dropped to the carpet and vigorously commenced his nightly routine of push-ups.

Paige stepped out of the shower to dry off. She wrapped a towel around her wet hair and tossed on her prim cotton nightgown. Over that she pulled her pink chenille robe. Thank God there was air-conditioning, she thought, though her heart was racing so badly she felt uncomfortably warm. At least she was well covered. She'd forgotten to pack her slippers when she'd left Florida, but there was nothing provocative about bare feet.

She smoothed moisturizer over her face with shaky fingers, then stood at the door. She strained to hear a sound that might give her a clue as to what Cooper was doing. Only a low murmur in a peculiar cadence penetrated the thin pressed wood.

Holding her breath, she exited the bathroom.

"One-twenty-five . . . one-twenty-six . . . one-twenty-seven. . . ." Cooper lost count of his push-ups when he caught sight of two slim bare feet. His hopeful gaze traveled upward, but collided against the hem of a long, fuzzy robe. Slowly he rose to his feet.

Paige crossed her arms in front of her, as if shielding her virtue. "I'm, uh, I'm finished. You can have it now." She cleared her throat. "The bathroom. You can have the bathroom now."

Cooper saw that her skin, always fair and smooth, now held a dewy blush. Tiny jewels of water clung to her throat and the sweet hollow at its base. The hot water of her shower would have made her body warm and rosy. She smelled clean and fresh and womanly.

Paige, her scent, her voice burned in Cooper's mind, inflamed his senses. Every receptor in his body screamed for her touch.

He watched her tug her robe more tightly around her. Paige was nervous, Cooper realized. Apprehensive. Why? Hadn't he proven she had nothing to fear from him?

She'd said she didn't want him. She'd told him to keep his distance.

Pride swept in, rushing through him like bitter venom.

By God, he'd keep his distance. She didn't have to worry on *that* account. He wasn't desperate. He'd never force himself on any woman, not even one who got to him the way Paige did.

And who was she trying to kid, anyway? She wanted him as much as he wanted her. She might look at him *now* with wide, anxious eyes, but he'd seen desire burning in them more than once. Oh, she wanted him, all right.

But he was a marine.

Warring emotions held him fast, swamping beliefs he'd always held as true. Family tradition. The Marine Corps. Destiny. These things had been drilled into him since before he could walk, before he could talk. And he'd never questioned his destiny. *He was supposed to be a marine.*

He wrenched free of his doubts and snatched up a pair of jeans from his case. He strode into the bathroom, thumping the door shut firmly behind him.

Cooper leaned back against the door, fists clenched. He didn't want a woman with no respect for heritage. Paige had none. Born and reared in the military community, she now rejected it. She rejected him.

He didn't want her. He didn't want her. He didn't want her.

She was poison.

Paige lay in her bed, covers pulled up around her chin, when she heard the bathroom door open. Cooper stepped out, and she found she couldn't look away. His tousled hair was damp, and his lean, hard body smelled of the soap he'd used—the same little bar she'd slid over her arms and thighs earlier. That thought caused a flutter in her middle.

Tawny hair dusted Cooper's chest and whorled around his navel, continuing its path below the boundary of denim, to an area best not imagined.

He didn't look at her. Instead, his face set in tight lines, he checked the locks on the door, then turned out the ancient overhead light. He walked down the narrow aisle between their beds.

As he stood close to her, Paige breathed in his clean manly scent, finding it curiously satisfying and exciting. From her pillow, she gazed up at jeans-clad thighs and a tightly curved posterior. Her heart's pace quickened. Under the blankets, her body stirred restlessly. She knew those two back pockets would be burned into her memory forever.

Cooper pulled back his own covers, but used only the sheet when he settled on the mattress. Without a word, he reached up and switched off the bedside lamp, casting the room into darkness.

Paige felt safer with the light off. He couldn't see her. More importantly, she couldn't see him. With a deep sigh, she snuggled into her bed, and closed her eyes.

The steady hum of the air conditioner filled the room.

Even though her body was exhausted from travel, heat, and tension, her mind refused to shut down. Sleep would not come.

There were so many things she didn't know about Cooper, so many things she wanted to know. She'd spent more time with him at close quarters than she'd ever spent with any man, and she didn't even know why he wanted to get to North Carolina in a hurry. What *did* she know about him, beyond his skill as a mechanic and his rank in the Marine Corps?

"Cooper?"

"What?" His clipped word told her he hadn't been sleeping, either.

She took a fortifying breath. "Cooper, why are you going to Jacksonville?"

He didn't reply immediately, and Paige knew with excruciating embarrassment she'd overstepped some invisible line. Just when she decided he wasn't going to answer, and she would never again ask him a personal question, he said, "My brother, Nathan, lives there. He manages our business. I think he's in trouble."

Relief flooded through Paige. She wanted to get to know Cooper. "Do you feel like talking about it?" she asked.

"There's not much to say. Someone's screwed up my credit. The only person who has access to my accounts, besides me, is Nathan, and I can't get in touch with him. We've been partners in Classics for three years and nothing like this has ever happened."

"Is there anyone else you could call? Your parents? A sister?"

She could hear him adjust his pillow. "My folks are in Okinawa. My dad's stationed there."

"Maybe your brother's called them. You know, for help. Maybe he's too embarrassed to come to you."

"No, Nathan wouldn't call Dad. It's understood that we're big boys now. Dad doesn't stick his nose into our business, and we don't drag him into our problems."

"Sort of an unwritten law?"

"Yeah."

It sounded extreme to Paige, such clear-cut uncrossable barriers between parents and sons. She found herself wondering if his parents had been any more concerned about their sons as children. Had new rules been drawn when Cooper and Nathan had reached manhood?

"Isn't there anyone else you could call?"

"No. Tomorrow I'll check again to see if he's left a message on my answering machine."

"What about your office? Would Nathan call there?"

"He hasn't so far."

"Cooper?"

"Hmm?"

"I . . . I want you to know how much I appreciate everything you've done for me."

He remained silent, and in the dark Paige burned in an agony of embarrassment.

Finally he spoke. "I should hope so."

She grabbed the extra pillow off of her bed and flung it where she guessed his head to be. A rich, baritone chuckle rewarded her, releasing a rabble of butterflies in her stomach.

"Sweet-tempered little wench." Humor warmed his words.

"You can be very trying, sometimes," she told him primly.

"I imagine so."

She tried to think of a suitable comeback, but couldn't. Cooper's side of the room went quiet, and she thought he might have drifted into sleep. She felt a twinge of disappointment. For the first time since she'd left Tipilo, Paige felt she had a friend.

His deep voice reached out to touch her. "So why are you in such a hurry to get to—where is it?—Plymouth, Florida?"

She found comfort in his question. "My cousin, Waldo—the one who gave me Henry—he's had a heart attack and he's in the hospital. He needs me."

"How old is Waldo?" Cooper asked. A peculiar timbre in his voice puzzled Paige.

"Eighty-four. I should never had gone to Arnold's."

"Arnold's?"

"Arnold is a friend of Waldo's. He and his son, Jeff, breed orchids, too."

"If Arnold is a friend of Waldo's, why didn't Waldo go?"

A shaft of moonlight fell across Cooper's bed, limning the angle of a wide shoulder, the masculine definition of an upper arm. Paige lost the thread of conversation. "Er, sorry?"

"I said, if Arnold is a friend of Waldo's, why didn't he go?"

"He wanted me to have the opportunity. You see, they've developed a new method of propagation. It's all very new." She wriggled up to lean back against the headboard and continued.

"I went to their operation in Tipilo to learn the technique. I worked in their greenhouses in exchange. I was getting the better end of the bargain, really, but Arnold and Waldo go way back."

"What do you hope to gain from this new method?" Cooper asked.

"We could bring up the production of Enchanted Orchids at relatively little cost. We need to do that because I've started exporting, and the demand for our flowers has doubled." She couldn't keep the trace of pride from her voice.

"And Waldo had a heart attack, so you're going home," Cooper concluded.

Paige hesitated. Was it wise to tell Cooper about the taxes? She wanted to. But he already thought her a little peculiar for dragging a hamster across country. She decided she wasn't ready to test his reaction.

"So," came his voice out of the dark, "you and Waldo are business partners?"

"Well, yes and no."

A pause. "I see."

"Technically, the business is mine. I'd already started Enchanted Orchids before Waldo arrived, and I'd bought the land it's on, along with my house. But Waldo has worked hard to make the business a success. I've offered to legally make him my partner, but he refused. He insists I keep what's mine. He says it's enough that he's got a roof over his head and family."

"Family."

Was that doubt in his voice? "I told you," Paige said, turning on her side to face the shadow shape in the other bed, "we're cousins."

"He's eighty-four years old and he's your *cousin?*"

Henry scratched around in his cage on the dresser.

"By degree—he's a distant cousin."

"I'll say."

"Family is family," she informed him tartly.

"Yeah," he agreed. Then, softly, "Whether you like it or not."

Paige heard his sheets rustle, and the moonbeam revealed he had turned on his side to face her. Dimly she could make out the shape of his head. From the tilt of it, his cheek must be resting against his hand, his bent elbow supporting the weight of his upper torso.

She no longer felt quite so hidden. Quite so safe. Pale lunar light slanted across a deep chest that tapered to a narrow waist. It illuminated a male nipple, ridged muscles, and the open, dull brass button of his jeans. Denim corners curled back to expose a small V of untanned skin bisected by a line of hair she knew must be rich brown. Her fingers tingled with the desire to touch. Dimly she became aware the conversation had faded. No words presented themselves for its renewal.

Cooper lost all inclination to talk. Instead he stared through the gloom, willing himself to see azure eyes, an elegant nose, and a sweet, ripe mouth that he knew, from the source of her voice, were facing him. Not four feet from him, Paige lay slim and soft under the sheets, and that knowledge edged him into a restless sweat. He rolled to his other side and nearly collided with the wall. Irritably he jerked at the covers. His cursed jeans felt tight and abrasive. He'd been a fool to worry about her sensibilities at the cost of his comfort. It was a mistake he wouldn't make again.

Her voice drifted over to him, soft and uncertain. "Good night, Cooper."

He hesitated in answering. He wanted to hurt her a little, but found he didn't have the heart. "Good night," he muttered grudgingly.

Squee-ak, squee-ak.

Chapter Six

Stars lingered in the dark morning sky as Paige and Cooper loaded up the car and drove away from the motel in search of breakfast.

"I thought I saw one of those twenty-four-hour places on our way in," Paige offered.

Cooper didn't answer. She didn't expect him to. Based on his grumpily lethargic behavior since her travel alarm had sounded, she'd come to the conclusion he was *not* a morning person.

The restaurant came into view. "Turn left here," Paige instructed.

Cooper turned the car into the driveway and stopped in the first empty parking space. When he made no move to get out, Paige gently took the keys from his fingers. Bloodshot amber eyes glared at her, and she barely managed to quell her laughter.

"Let's go inside, Cooper," she coaxed. "Coffee."

"I'm not an idiot," he growled. "I know there's coffee in there."

"Then come on." She got out and came around to open his door.

His scowl grew more fierce at her courtesy. "What do you plan to do with the rat?"

She picked up her sweater and draped it over Henry's cage. "The same thing we did in the grocery store and the Western Union office and the bank."

"I was afraid of that."

As they walked inside and were led to a table, Paige kept close to Cooper, using his body as a shield to hide Henry. Once they slid into their booth, she placed the cage against the wall, and lifted just enough of her sweater to ensure the hamster's comfort. Carefully she added the extra camouflage of her purse.

When the waitress came, Paige ordered coffee for them both. They studied their menus in silence as they waited.

Glancing up to see if he'd made his selection yet, she noticed the dark smudges under Cooper's eyes. So his night had been less than restful, she thought with satisfaction. At least she wasn't the only one who hadn't gotten much sleep.

Misery loved company.

Cooper slapped the large, glossy menu down on the table, looking decidedly bad-tempered. At that moment the waitress arrived with a carafe of coffee. She scribbled their orders on her pad and left.

Paige smiled as she poured for Cooper. He mumbled his thanks and took a long draw of the hot stuff. She poured a cupful for herself, and, sipping leisurely, sat back to watch for a transformation.

It didn't start until the second cup. It accelerated with the first few bites of his pancakes and eggs, and was complete by the time he popped the last morsel of toast into his mouth.

Paige recalled the previous morning. He'd slept hours later, maybe that accounted for the difference in alertness. Or maybe it was two sleepless nights in a row, with a trying day in between. Tomorrow morning would tell.

But first they'd have to get through another night together.

The internal havoc that thought caused disturbed Paige. Cooper had been a perfect gentleman last evening, so what was she concerned about?

The answer was too easy, and she didn't like it one bit.

Resolutely she gulped the rest of her coffee, and set the cup down. "Are you ready to go?" Even to her own ears her voice sounded defensive.

Cooper raised an eyebrow. "Just waiting on you, sugar. You seemed to be thinking."

She picked up the bill. "Let's hit the road, Angelsmith." After counting out a tip for the waitress, Paige went to the register to pay for their meals.

Outside she reminded him they had to stop at the grocery store to replenish the cooler.

"Tucson is only about fifty miles from here," Cooper pointed out. "We can get supplies there while we let the car cool down."

Paige nodded. In Tucson she'd call Maggie. In Tucson they could also look for a junkyard.

Paige cringed inwardly as the driver behind them gunned his engine and pulled into the left lane, roaring past them with an angry glare. She knew she'd have to get used to the rudeness of motorists who took exception to the slow pace Cooper and she had to keep.

She studied his profile for a moment. Never talkative, he seemed even quieter than usual. It was as if Cooper's body moved on autopilot while his mind dwelled a million miles away.

With a small sigh she gazed through the window at miles of gold and red earth flecked with hardy scrub grass and cacti. Here and there sparse bushes bloomed a vivid yellow. Mountains loomed in the near distance.

The scenery failed to soothe her. Her thoughts churned with worry for Waldo and Maggie, for Enchanted Orchids and her home. And she was too aware of Cooper. His presence pressed in on her in the closeness of the car. She looked for a distraction and finally reached for the knob on the radio.

"Please don't turn that on."

Paige jumped at the sound of Cooper's voice. Below dark glasses his white teeth flashed in a smile.

"I thought some music might help pass the time," she said.

"Have mercy. I've heard enough mariachi music to last me the rest of my life."

She couldn't repress a smile of her own. "Maybe it's an acquired taste. I'll look for something else."

"I don't care if you get Tiny Tim's greatest hits, just, please, no mariachi."

"Okay, I promise. If that's all I can find, I'll turn the radio off."

They settled on Tammy Wynette's "Stand By Your Man," and sang along in exaggerated twanging accents the few lyrics they knew.

"Whoo-ee, gal," Cooper exclaimed when the song ended. "Yore gud!"

Paige lowered her eyes demurely. "Oh, pishaw."

They continued to serenade the radio until a battered double-wide trailer came into view, miles distant from the highway. In the front "yard" sat an old car, stripped of its tires and doors. Behind the trailer squatted a dilapidated wooden shed. Less than half a mile away, a stucco house sported its own rusting monument, a tractor. The few other homesteads gave equal testimony to a harsh environment and harsher fate.

"Oh, look," Paige muttered. "Civilization." She'd seen similar neglect in Plymouth, but it had never looked as bleak. There, lush foliage grew up to conceal the hard edges of poverty.

Cooper's sharp oath snagged her attention. He slowed and pulled the car onto the shoulder of the highway.

"What?" she asked. "What's wrong?" She leaned over and checked the instruments. The idiot light shone like an evil beacon. Quickly she glanced toward the hood. "But there's no steam," she protested.

"It might not be the radiator," Cooper told her, opening his door and stepping out. He retrieved the rag from under his seat and then lifted the hood.

Paige scooted to the driver's side. She wanted to ask him what the problem was, but decided against it. He had enough to cope with; he didn't need any distractions from her. She came to stand quietly beside him.

He glanced at her. "I don't suppose you happen to have a spare fan belt in the trunk?"

She worried her bottom lip between her teeth and looked from the car's machinery to Cooper's face.

"I didn't think so," he muttered. He released a harsh sigh.

"Can't you make one out of a-a belt? Or—" her face grew hot "—a...bra?" She'd read somewhere of a bra being used in a desperate moment.

His bark of laughter made her wish she'd kept her mouth shut.

"A *bra?*" he echoed incredulously. "Is this some closely guarded secret in Detroit? 'Don't let the people know they can use bras or we'll never sell another fan belt'?"

"It was just a suggestion!"

Cooper eyed her speculatively. "You volunteering yours?" he asked. He held out his open hand, palm up. "Come on, give it here. I'm willing to try anything once."

"Just forget I said anything," she snapped.

"Look." He directed her attention to three wheels attached to the engine. "The belt fits around these pulleys. It's got to be tight, because it moves about a thousand miles a minute. Do you think a bra would *fit* in there, much less stand the stress and wear?"

"Okay, what about a belt?"

"The same thing applies. What have you got against using a real fan belt, anyway? If you want, we'll try a bra or a belt. See how far it gets us. Right now we're within walking distance of houses where we can probably get help. But when that jury-rigged belt snaps, assuming it would work at all, where will we be? Maybe out in the middle of nowhere. You want to chance it?"

Paige glared off into the distance. "I was just trying to help."

Cooper reached out to touch her shoulder, but dropped his hand before he made contact. "I know you were," he said, his tone now softer, almost tender. "Look, you stay here with the car and I'll hike over to one of those houses we passed and see if I can scare up a fan belt or a telephone."

"I'll come with you," she offered hopefully. She was tired of sitting by the side of the road in a hot, broken-down car.

This time Cooper did place his hands on her shoulders, and he steered her away from the hood to the front seat. "I think it would be better if you stayed. Besides, you can't leave your pet rodent—"

"Henry," she corrected.

"—here. He'll die." Cooper locked gazes with her. "Look, I don't like leaving you alone like this, but it's got to be over a hundred degrees out and those houses are at least five miles away." He went to the trunk and poured a large paper cup full of water; they had no canteen.

"I can make it," she insisted. "I'm in good shape, really I am."

His expression tightened. "I'm sure you are."

"I'll bring Henry. His cage is very light. Cooper—" She stopped and drew a breath. "Cooper, I'm coming with you," she said firmly.

"All right."

For an instant she stared at him, surprised. "All right? Just like that?"

"I didn't want to leave you here, anyway," he muttered.

Pleased, Paige dug through her luggage and presented him with her fluorescent pink, fold-up umbrella. "We can take this. It'll help keep the sun off us. We don't want to get sunstroke."

"You took an umbrella to Southern California in the summer?"

She checked Henry's water dispenser, then filled a cup for herself. "I've lived in Florida so long I automatically pack an umbrella."

Cooper locked the car and smiled at her. "Well, I'm glad you do, even if your choice of color is . . . *this.*"

Paige smiled back at him, taking comfort from his presence. "Next time I'll pack basic black." She dropped a T-shirt over Henry's cage.

"Ready?"

She nodded. "As I'll ever be."

They clambered down the incline from the highway, setting sand and pebbles tumbling. From their new vantage point, the houses looked discouragingly farther away.

"It's not too late to go back and stay with the car," Cooper offered.

Paige pushed her sunglasses back into place on her nose. "You'd probably get lost without me. I'd never forgive myself." She flashed him an impish grin.

"Yeah. Right. C'mon, scout." Cooper popped open the umbrella, and they started off across the desert.

They walked over an hour before the homesteads seemed any closer. It didn't take that long for Paige to realize Cooper would have made better time without her. His longer legs were capable of eating up the distance. But he never complained, never implied she was slowing him down. He adjusted their pace to one that was comfortable for her. After they reached the unpaved road that appeared to lead to the group of houses, they made better time.

The wind gusted, scouring them with grit. Insects took up an ear-piercing whine.

Cooper increased his speed and hastened Paige along with an occasional guiding touch of his hand to her back or shoulder.

Clouds as dark as caldrons swept in to roil overhead, and Cooper relentlessly urged her to greater haste. A painful stitch nagged her side, but she jogged faster.

Suddenly light shattered in the ominous clouds and scribbled down to spear the earth in a half dozen terrifying strokes.

Paige screamed as lightning struck twenty yards to her left.

"Run!" Cooper barked.

Thunder boomed as she flew down the road, legs churning.

Lightning forked down again, surrounding the runners, motivating them to ignore fatigue and pain. Thunder rolled out over the desert. Bullets of water exploded against their skin, drenching them in seconds. The barrage cloaked the land in a hard veil of gray, obscuring their squinted vision. Battered by water, they struggled on.

Paige wrapped her arms around Henry's cage to shield him as much as possible, but she was afraid the tiny animal wouldn't survive long in this downpour. Where were those damned houses?

Then she felt Cooper's hand grip her wrist, pulling her toward a blurred hulk. As they neared the form, she recognized the trailer.

A flimsy awning provided little protection as Cooper banged nonstop on the aluminum door. Paige watched, huddled over Henry, afraid Cooper might try to break the door down, afraid he might not. His clothes were plastered to his body, his hair slicked to his skull. He narrowed his eyes against the rain, his dark lashes spiked, his eyebrows drawn down in a fierce scowl.

No one answered.

"C'mon," Cooper shouted over the roar of the rain. He took her hand, and together they ran across the gravel yard and down the road.

A quarter of a mile farther they found a house. A tall, slim, young man answered the first crash of Cooper's fist. Quickly he pulled them inside, slamming the door closed. "Wait here," he instructed, then disappeared down the hall to return seconds later with towels.

Chests heaving to drag in oxygen, Cooper and Paige scrubbed and blotted towels over drenched skin, dripping hair and saturated clothing.

"Thanks," Cooper said. "I thought we were going to drown."

"What were you doing outside, anyway?" the young man asked.

"Our car lost a fan belt on I-10. We were on our way here for help when the storm caught us."

Paige was conscious of the two men stopping their conversation to watch her as she knelt by the cage and coaxed a wet, indignant Henry into her hand. She rescued him from floating wood chips, to cradle him in her cupped palms. Gently she dried him with the corner of her towel.

"A *hamster?* You brought a hamster with you?" the young man exclaimed incredulously. "By the way, I'm Donald Amery."

"Cooper Angelsmith. Paige Ruegger." The men shook hands, but Donald's attention remained glued to Henry.

"Yeah," Cooper said, "the rodent's sort of a…mascot."

Henry climbed over Paige's thumb to fix his black stare on the marine. His body quivered as if enraged at being labeled a mere mascot. With aloof dignity, the hamster slowly turned his back on Cooper and proceeded to groom bedraggled fur.

With their host's permission, Paige emptied the contents of the cage into a lined trash can in the utility area behind the kitchen.

He handed her a section of newspaper to shred for a new lining. "My phone's not working. Must be the storm. As soon as it's over I'm going to check on my sister, Cindy. Afterward, I'll take you to Earl's gas station. He'll have a fan belt for you."

"Is your sister ill?" Paige asked.

Donald chuckled. "Well, she *has* been. Mostly she's just real pregnant. Her husband, Roy, is in Okinawa. He's a marine."

"Another marine," she muttered.

"What?"

Paige found herself face-to-face with the innocence of Donald's blond, blue-eyed youth. "Cooper's a marine."

"Really?" The light of hero worship glimmered in Donald's eyes as he regarded the older man. "You been to Okinawa?"

"Yes. My father's there now."

"Mind if I ask you some questions?"

By the time the storm blew over, and everyone squeezed into the cab of Donald's battered pickup truck, Paige had heard all about the opportunities for training and travel the Corps offered. She'd also learned Cooper was a graduate of Annapolis. As they bumped along the road that wound up into the mountains, Donald's eager grilling also revealed the Angelsmith tradition of the first-born son making his career in the Marine Corps—a tradition that dated back to the Quasi-War with France in the eighteenth century.

Paige turned her head to gaze blindly out the window. What did it matter to her if Cooper's family bound themselves to almost two hundred years of military tradition?

Nothing. Nothing at all.

Donald pulled into the driveway of a trim little house. A birdfeeder held the place of honor in the front yard, surrounded by faded, yellow plastic flowers stuck in the ground.

"That's funny," Donald said, his blond eyebrows pulling down. "Her front door is open. Cindy never leaves her doors open—the house is air-conditioned."

Before Cooper could stop Donald from running straight into an unknown situation, the young man jumped out of the cab and flew across the yard. With an oath, Cooper quickly followed, Paige on his heels.

A nerve-rending scream assaulted them as they burst through the doorway.

"Cindy!" Donald cried, and raced through the house.

They found her panting on her bed, pale and frightened. "Donny?" she whimpered. "Oh, Donny, thank God you're here. I was out filling the birdfeeder when ... the pain...wet..." She reached out for him, grasping his hand "The baby's coming!"

Donald paled. "No! It can't! It's not due for another two weeks."

Cooper and Paige had held back to allow them privacy Now Paige moved into the small room. "Have you called the doctor?" She recognized panic in both brother and sister and worked to control her own. "We need to get Cindy to the hospital."

"Phone's been out for hours," the young woman supplied, regaining her breath. "The hospital is too far, so Roy and I made arrangements for a midwife who lives much closer."

"It's time to go get her," Paige said. "Donald, do you know where she is?"

"Yeah." His worried gaze remained on his sister's face.

Paige sympathized with him, but action was called for. "If you give me directions, I'll go get the midwife."

Donald frowned. "You'd never find her. You don't know these mountain roads."

Above all, Paige did *not* want to stay here. But it looked as if there was no choice. "Then go."

"Okay." Donald took a deep breath and let it out. "Okay." He directed a tormented look to his sister. "Cindy, honey, you hang in there. I'll be right back. And don't you worry. Paige . . . Paige, here, will take care of everything."

Everything. Paige swallowed hard.

Donald ran from the house.

Cooper bolted after him.

Paige caught up with Cooper before he made it to the front door. She grabbed his arm and hung on like a terrier. "Where do you think you're going?" she demanded in a low, furious voice.

"With Don!"

"Oh, no, you aren't." Paige clung tighter when he tried to shake her off. "You're not leaving me here alone with Cindy, you weasel! Donald can find the midwife just fine, but that woman in there needs you. *I* need you. I don't know anything about labor and babies."

"Look." Cooper licked his dry lips. "You don't need me here. I'd only get in the way." He tried to pry her fingers from his arm. "This is woman stuff! Hell, my father was stationed overseas when I was born and my mother made it through okay."

Cindy moaned.

Panic and anger surged through Paige, giving her new strength. She dropped her hands to her sides and stepped back. "Another great military tradition," she sneered. "Never being there when your wife needs you. Did you ever ask how your mother felt? Was she frightened? A young woman going through childbirth for the first time and her mate—the man whose child she was bearing, the man who'd promised to love, honor, and protect her—was gone. As usual." She spun around and dashed back to Cindy's room.

Outside, the engine of the ancient truck cranked up, and tires spat gravel.

Cindy's face contorted in pain, and a scream took form deep in her throat. Without thinking, Paige wiped her sweaty palms on her jeans and clasped the suffering woman's hand. Cindy gripped her as if she'd offered a lifeline.

Cooper quietly reentered the room. He took Cindy's other hand. "Breathe! In and out, fast. Puff, puff, puff. Do it!"

Cindy tried but she was already too deep in the contraction to catch her breath.

Paige glanced up to meet Cooper's eyes. A brief, silent message passed between them. Apology and welcome. As one, they turned their attention back to Cindy.

Gradually her agony eased.

Paige leaned forward and smoothed back sweat-soaked hair from a white cheek. "I'm going to get you a nice cool cloth for your face, Cindy. I'll be right back."

Her eyes widened. "Please don't leave me."

Paige gave her most reassuring smile. "I'm not leaving. I'm only going to get a cold cloth for you. Cooper is here. Did you know he's a marine?"

Along with the moist cloth, Paige brought back ice chips. She slipped one between Cindy's dry lips. Gently, Cooper cooled the young woman's face with the cloth.

Abruptly her face twisted in pain. Cooper coached her. Together they breathed, fast and shallow. At one point her pain gurgled through, but it finally receded, and Cooper showed Cindy how to taper off and resume normal respiration.

Paige murmured encouragement, watching in amazement. Was this the Cooper who had tried to follow Donald out the door? The same Cooper who conducted a running feud with a hamster? Cooper Angelsmith, morning grouch?

"How do you know so much about contractions and breathing?" Cindy asked him. "Did you do this with your wife?" She turned her eyes to Paige, who remembered in the confusion of discovering Cindy's plight, there had been no last names mentioned.

Cooper refused to worry the expectant mother by telling her he'd gained his limited knowledge from a television comedy series. Hell, he worked with bulk fuel, not babies. He looked at Paige, who managed a smile. "Yes," he lied.

"Was seeing your baby born the most beautiful experience of your life?" Cindy's eyes pleaded with them.

He didn't hesitate a second. "Yes, it was. I'll never forget. It was absolutely... beautiful. Wasn't it, dear?" He looked at Paige meaningfully.

"Uh, beautiful. Yes, indeed. I'll never forget it... darling."

Tears welled in Cindy's brown eyes. "I wish Roy was here," she whispered. "Our first child."

"I know he wishes he was here," Cooper assured her as he applied a re-moistened cloth to her face. But wishing wasn't good enough, was it? Roy was overseas. Strangers comforted his wife and would see his first child born.

Paige offered Cindy an ice chip. "Just think about holding your baby in your arms. Your baby."

The contractions came harder and closer together. Cooper fretted at Donald's delay. He'd been gone two hours. Was it normal for labor to continue this long? Should Cindy be in this much pain? If something wasn't going right, neither he nor Paige would know it. And they wouldn't know how to cope with a problem if there was one.

"Something's changing," Cindy panted.

"What?" Paige asked anxiously. "What's different?"

"Pressure."

With the next contraction, Cindy began to push. Over her head, Cooper caught Paige's look. *Oh, God,* it said.

After the contraction finished, Paige asked Cindy where the sheets were kept, and went to fetch two. Next she went to the kitchen and checked on the water she'd set to boil earlier. She located a pair of kitchen scissors in a drawer, washed them and dropped them into the pot.

Where was that midwife?

Paige hurried back to Cindy, clutching the sheets. With a smile she hoped looked more confident than she felt, she brushed back a damp lock of hair from Cindy's forehead. "Bend your knees, Cindy, and I'll drape this sheet over them."

Earlier, when Cooper had been out of the room, Paige had helped Cindy out of her wet clothing into a modest cotton nightgown.

Now Paige slipped one sheet under Cindy's bottom, spreading the clean percale out to the end of the bed. The second sheet she draped over the other woman's bent knees, pushing the hem of the nightgown clear of the birth area.

Cindy shot a wild look at Cooper, who stood near her shoulder, holding her sweating hand. He'd discreetly turned in an effort to preserve as much of her modesty as possible. She turned that same look on Paige. "The midwife isn't going to make it, is she?"

"We don't know," Paige said quietly.

Sweating and straining, Cindy continued to bear down with each contraction. Her strength drained lower and lower.

Paige chewed on her lip and worried.

Another contraction seized the young woman. She panted and grunted.

"Cindy!" Paige cried, amazed, shaken. "I can see your baby's head!" At least, she hoped it was the baby's head.

The mother's eyes widened with mingled joy and relief. She drew a breath and pushed harder.

Cooper's wide, wavering grin told Paige he was caught between elation and disbelief. His amber eyes lifted from Cindy's face to Paige's.

They were witness to a miracle and, at that moment, Paige wanted to share her fear and wonderment with Cooper as she'd never wanted to share anything with any man before.

But this was Cindy's moment, and Paige determined that if the young mother couldn't have her husband there, she would at least have the undivided attention of those who were present.

"Oh, God! Here comes a shoulder!" Paige's existence telescoped to the small, red being emerging into the world. Cindy's daughter finally slipped into Paige's waiting, shaking hands.

The front door banged open. Donald cried, "Cindy!"

The midwife walked into the room as the baby gave its first wail.

As the older woman took over, a tangle of emotions swamped Paige. Relief, elation, envy, and others she could not define rioted within her, leaving her confused and frighteningly vulnerable. She tried to sort through them but all she could think of was that small, red, wrinkled baby she'd held in her hands.

"Paige." Cindy's call was little more than a whisper, and she quickly stepped to the new mother's side.

Cindy's smile was pale and tired, but an underlying radiance shone through. "Thank you. Thank you, both." Her gaze slid across the room to where Cooper stood alone. "I think he needs you now."

Paige walked toward him. In his dark gold eyes she read a bleakness that made her ache for him. She slipped her arms around his waist and held him close, her cheek pressed to his chest.

Instantly his arms encircled her in a fierce embrace, but his eyes remained fixed on the baby, swaddled now in a soft blanket as Cindy accepted her daughter from the midwife.

"My father missed this," he said, his voice low and raw.

She wanted to comfort him. "When you were born, they probably wouldn't have allowed your father to be present during delivery."

Cooper shook his head. "He missed the first year."

"Oh."

"My grandfather missed this three times."

The midwife came over to congratulate them and to explain that a complicated birth accounted for her delay; Paige could tell he barely listened. His mind was occupied with something else.

Cooper approached the newborn with obvious trepidation, but he seemed unable to resist some invisible pull.

"What are you going to name her?" he asked Cindy as he gazed down at the sleeping infant.

But exhaustion had overcome Cindy. Her chest rose and fell in the rhythm of deep slumber.

Paige looked back at Cooper, and what she saw stilled her summons on her tongue.

Cooper Angelsmith, Captain, USMC, reached out a hesitant finger to stroke a tiny pink fist.

And melted Paige's heart.

Chapter Seven

The ride from Earl's Service Station was a quiet one. Donald seemed wrapped in his own thoughts, and Cooper spoke not one word. Paige possessed neither the will nor the energy to carry on a conversation.

She wanted a private place to sort out her feelings. She needed to regain control of at least that fraction of her life, and it frightened her that she seemed unable to cope with even that.

Warm fingers laced through hers. She glanced up at Cooper, but he continued to gaze straight ahead through the windshield. The only response she received was a light squeeze.

Paige found the gesture oddly soothing. Maybe, just maybe, he needed the contact as much as she did. She acknowledged their link with a squeeze of her own.

Donald pulled up behind the car still parked on the side of the highway, baking in the heat. He refused to leave until Cooper had replaced the fan belt with one of the two he'd picked up at Earl's. Cindy's grateful brother had insisted on paying for the belts. Now, as Donald watched Cooper start the car, he wished them well, profuse with thanks.

Hot, dry air whipped through the open windows as Paige and Cooper headed toward Tucson. For the first time since the long ordeal had begun, she realized how tired and hungry she was. She slumped in the seat. "I'm starved."

His eyes flicked down to his watch, then back to the road. "No wonder. The last food we ate was this morning. It's past dinnertime now."

"We're both tired and hungry. Let's stop for the night in Tucson," she suggested.

She thought of Waldo and Maggie, of Enchanted Orchids, and of taxes. A full day's travel had been lost.

It was the measure of Cooper's exhaustion that he agreed with no argument. "All right," he said. "We'll get something to eat then find a motel."

"Grocery store?"

"That can wait until tomorrow. I'm not prepared to smuggle a rat into a decent, unsuspecting business right now."

"Henry is not a rat," she protested tiredly.

"How does a burger, fries, and a chocolate shake sound to you?"

"Like high livin'."

"Can't we afford it?" he asked, concentrating on the traffic approaching through the dusk. He switched on the headlights, then hooked his wrist over the steering wheel.

"Yeah. We just can't make a habit of it."

"So tomorrow we'll buy groceries."

When they arrived in Tucson, Cooper took the exit onto Speedway Boulevard, and from there they finally located a

Burger Prince. While he ordered for them, Paige found a telephone and called Maggie.

"Where you been, child?" the older woman demanded anxiously. "Everything all right?"

"Yes, Maggie. I'm alive and well in Tucson, Arizona."

"Tucson? Let's see . . ." There was a rustle of heavy paper. "According to my map, you didn't get very far. Car trouble?"

"Of course. The fan belt broke and Cooper and I had to hike for help. How's Waldo, Maggie? How are you?"

Maggie's smile came through her words. "Waldo's raisin' cane with the nurses. Fussin' all the time. He wants to come home, but they won't let him. Too unstable, they say.

"Now, what's this about you and the marine hikin' for help? No wonder you sound so tired."

Paige leaned back against the restaurant wall. "That's not the half of it. Maggie, we delivered a baby."

There was a second's silence on the other end of the line.

"I thought you said you delivered a baby."

Paige chuckled. "I did. The sister of the man who helped us. She was alone—her husband is overseas—and a storm knocked her phone out. The midwife was on another emergency call, so that left Cooper and me."

"Well, I've delivered a few babies in my time. Nothin' like it in the world. Holdin' that squallin' pruny little thing, you think it's prettier than anything you've ever seen. And you wish it was yours."

Paige swallowed. "Yeah," she agreed hoarsely. "You sure do."

Maggie's voice softened. "Your turn'll come, girl. When you find the right man, your turn'll come."

Cooper closed the motel room door, flipping the dead bolt.

He'd hoped a brisk walk around the Desert Diamond Motel would help release some of his mounting tension. It hadn't. Now the steady sound of water running through the pipes told him Paige was in the shower, and the erotic mental images that assailed him sent him looking for a burn of another kind. Cooper dropped to the carpet and began counting off push-ups.

In the shower, Paige rinsed her hair. As the hot water sluiced over her body, images streamed through her mind's eye. Cooper working under the car's hood; Cooper pounding on the trailer door in the gray waterfall of rain; Cooper touching the baby's hand.

"Cooper." She said his name aloud, enjoying the sound of it. Thinking about the man brought her even greater pleasure. Thoughtful, sexy, competent enough to handle any situation fortune threw his way. Cooper Angelsmith was a very special man.

But he was a marine.

Anguish twisted her middle, tightened her throat. She didn't want him to be a marine. She wanted him to be someone she could allow herself to care about. Even though they had only a short time together before they reached their destination and went their separate ways, Paige knew it would be easy to love Cooper. He was someone rare, someone wonderful, and she didn't know if anyone like him would ever pass through her life again.

Cooper rose from the carpet when he heard the bathroom door open. Face averted, Paige tried to hurry by him.

"Your turn," she muttered.

He frowned. Something was wrong. "Paige?"

She stood facing her bed, head bowed, her back to him.

"Paige?" He took the few steps that separated them and gently caught her arm, turning her toward him. She refused to meet his gaze. With a crooked forefinger, he nudged her chin up. "What's wrong?" She kept her eyes lowered. "Talk to me, Paige," he coaxed softly.

"Nothing to talk about," she told him in a small voice.

The clean smell of her, the newly-scrubbed freshness of her soft skin, her very closeness made Cooper a little lightheaded. Without thinking, he took a step closer. Unable to resist any longer, in spite of Paige's reticence, he lowered his head and touched his mouth to hers.

Paige knew wisdom dictated she resist him, shut him out of her heart, but all she could think of was his gentleness. He kissed her with such piercing tenderness she hurt. Hesitantly she rested her palms against his chest, making contact with the knit cotton that covered masculine hair-dusted skin, hard muscle and bone.

Cooper's large, fine hands came up to splay softly against her back, guiding her closer to his warm man's body. Lost in the magic of his kiss, she came to him.

His mouth grew more demanding, drawing her into deeper intimacy. With little coaxing from him, she parted her lips, inviting exploration by his tongue.

Passion, sudden and hot, seared through her. Paige clutched her fingers in his thick, cropped hair. She wanted Cooper.

He made a low sound of desire in his throat as his breathing grew shallower, faster, and his arms tightened around her. He moved his hands up and down her back.

She wanted to feel his hands on her naked breasts. She wanted to feel the weight of him on her, the male strength of him inside her. She needed him. Now.

Caught in the thick fog of her desire, Paige stumbled over reason.

She wanted Cooper. But she didn't want a military man. Not a soldier. Not a sailor. Especially not a marine. She didn't want to spend chunks of her life waiting. And worrying. She refused to live like her mother had.

Paige swallowed a surge of emotion as the likelihood of her being just a passing fancy to Cooper struck home. His words echoed in her mind.

It'll take more than one night to get to Florida. I wasn't proposing. I'm open to a little fun, and you're not.

Cooper sensed Paige's withdrawal before she could ease away from him. Still breathing hard, he studied her face. Shuttered, wide-spaced eyes the color of summer returned his gaze. Her lush mouth, swollen from his kisses, was unsmiling.

"What is it, Paige?"

She wanted to find a private place and vent her grief. But there wasn't such a place, not while she traveled with Cooper. It was up to her to create her own barriers.

"I'm still not open to a little fun, leatherneck."

Cooper felt as if she'd struck him. The pain her invisible blow inflicted caught him off guard. He covered his weakness quickly. "Pity. You might have learned something." With savage satisfaction he watched color stain her cheeks.

Without another word, he turned and sauntered into the bathroom, closing the door behind him. He turned on the shower and welcomed the heat. In minutes the small room filled with billowing steam.

He was a fool.

She'd been honest with him from the start.

He lowered his head under the punishing needle-fine spray.

Who would have thought he'd be so attracted to a stubborn, sunburned woman with wild, wind-blown hair and rumpled clothing? But he was. He found her incredibly sexy. Cooper scoured his skin with the rough, soapy wash-cloth, as if he could wash away his desire for Paige along with the sweat and grime.

Paige. She was a real trooper. Willing to do what needed to be done—someone a man could depend on. That was important in a marine's uncertain life. It was important in any man's life.

But she wasn't for him, she'd made that clear.

No matter how he felt about her, she wasn't for him.

"Ready?" Paige asked, her gaze fixed on Henry's cage, which she held in front of her.

Cooper fitted the last suitcase into the car, and shut the trunk more firmly than the creaky hinges warranted. "Ready," he answered tightly.

He wanted to grab her by the shoulders and shake her. She'd limited her conversation to basics, which normally he would have preferred this early in the day. This morning it annoyed him. But what grated on his nerves was her refusal to meet his eyes. As if, he thought irritably, she feared her mere glance would inflame him.

He slid into the passenger seat and Paige started the car. She pulled out onto the road, but to his surprise, headed in the opposite direction of the interstate.

"Where are you going?" he asked. "I-10 is that way."

She kept her gaze on the road ahead. "I know. But the motel manager gave me directions to a big junkyard. I thought we could find a place to eat on the way."

Cooper scowled. He hadn't had his breakfast, not even a cup of coffee, and this difficult woman was changing their schedule. It was indecent. Against his better judgment, he asked, "Junkyard?"

Still she didn't look at him, and his annoyance ground up a notch.

Finally she answered. "You said we'd get another radiator."

At that moment they spotted a twenty-four-hour restaurant, and Paige turned into its parking lot. Once again she smuggled Henry in.

Other than the words necessary to place their orders with the waitress, neither Cooper nor Paige spoke.

Paige avoided looking at Cooper. She'd treated him so badly last night she wasn't sure she'd ever be able to meet his eyes again. As soon as the words had left her mouth, she had wished them back. She'd hurt Cooper. She'd seen it in that instant before he'd brought his guard up. The knowledge was like a knife slicing at her heart.

She fiddled with a package of sweetener as she considered how wrong she'd been. She'd lied to him and tried hard to believe the lie herself. But she couldn't. Paige swallowed against the remorse thickening in her throat. Unfortunately, Cooper had believed her lie. He had believed he was nothing more to her than a marine on the make.

The waitress brought their food, and they ate in silence. After Cooper finally placed his knife and fork across his empty plate, Paige forced herself to look at him.

She found no anger in the lines and planes of his handsome face, no sadness. In fact, she found no emotion at all. As Cooper sipped his coffee, he regarded her over the rim of the cup. His amber eyes, so capable of making a woman feel caressed, now remained shuttered. Paige swallowed again. It was better this way, she told herself.

Paige took a deep breath and quietly let it out. There was nothing left to do but get on with the business of getting home. The sooner the better. "About the radiator..."

"Yes, what about the radiator?" he drawled.

"Well," she said, folding the corner of her still unused package of sweetener, "you said it would be a good idea to change the one in the car. That we could find a new one at the junkyard. Well—" she cleared her throat, still staring at the small paper package "—I got directions to a junkyard from the motel manager this morning."

"Good thinking."

Unable to determine whether or not that was sarcasm she heard in his voice, Paige looked up. "You did say it would be a good idea to change the radiator," she insisted defensively.

"'A good idea'? Those were my exact words?"

"Maybe not your *exact* words, but the meaning's the same."

"No," he said bluntly. "It is *not* a good idea. And I never mentioned the word 'good', because there's not a damn thing good about it."

"You said—"

"Don't tell me what I said. What I'm saying *now* is that trying to replace the radiator is a bad idea, today."

"Why?" She set her jaw and glared at him. He *had* said the radiator needed to be changed.

He took another sip of his coffee and set down the cup. "We lost almost a full day's travel yesterday. If I try to change radiators, we'll lose another entire day, maybe more."

"You said to trust you," she accused.

Something blazed in his eyes. "And you've done an excellent job of it, haven't you?"

Paige flinched. She'd hurt him last night, and she was paying for it now. "I trust you," she said patiently.

He leaned toward her and his voice was low and fierce. "No you don't. You don't even trust yourself, do you, sugar? Especially not with some big bad marine. But don't worry. You're safe from me. I won't bother you again."

Tears stung the back of Paige's eyes. "Cooper, I—"

His open hand cut the air in an angry gesture of denial, cutting off her words. He thumped back in his seat and stared over her head for a long moment.

"I did say I'd change the radiator," he said quietly. "But I gave it some thought afterward. I don't have a place to work, and I don't have the proper tools. At the very least we'd lose another full day. There's a good chance it would take longer."

"But we could make it up. We'd be able to go faster."

"We'd have to go the speed of light to make up two days."

Cooper could see she doubted him. But what was new? "Okay, we'll go to the junkyard and see what they have." What had ever made him believe she might trust him? He wasn't a civilian.

While Paige paid for their breakfast, Cooper found a pay telephone and called his office at Camp Pendleton to see if his brother had left a message. He was stunned when he was given a phone number, left the day before. Quickly he wrote it down.

After he hung up, he studied the number. It was unfamiliar.

What was going on? Was Nathan in the hospital?

Cooper dialed the number his brother had left for him.

There was caution in Nathan's voice. "Hello?"

"Nathe."

"Cooper! Where are you?" Nathan demanded, relief coloring his words.

"I'm standing at a pay phone in Tucson, Arizona, without a credit card or check that wouldn't bounce sky-high. Where the hell have *you* been, little brother?" Anxiety for

Nathan surged, fueling the simmering anger. Cooper gripped the receiver. "What the hell is going on!"

"It—it's a long story. What are you doing in Tucson? Why aren't you at Pendleton?" Nathan's voice sounded strained and slightly hoarse, as if he'd been doing a lot of talking lately.

Cooper clamped down on his temper. "I'm on my way to Jacksonville," he said evenly. "I've been calling you for four days. There's no answer at Classics, and at your place all I get is the machine. I'm broke, Nathan, and I want to know what happened to all my money."

"It's... I..." Nathan released a ragged sigh. "Coop, I'm sorry. I haven't got the head for business you do. You've always been *good* at this, and I... haven't. I've tried. For three years I've tried my damnedest. No excuses, Coop. Classics is in trouble and it's my fault."

Cooper closed his eyes against the frustration and worry that gnawed at his stomach. The business he'd started and nurtured, before reluctantly turning it over to his younger brother to run, was in jeopardy. His creation, Cooper's Classics, had provided him with more challenge, more enjoyment, more profound satisfaction than anything else in his life. What had started as a lark had grown into the focus of his future. And now his brother was telling him something was wrong, very wrong, with that cherished dream.

He leaned back against the restaurant wall, pinching the bridge of his nose between a thumb and forefinger. "What happened?"

"I'm just not any good at business, Coop—"

"*What happened!*"

There was a pause. Then Nathan said tightly, "I changed suppliers and paid too much for parts. I tried to expand Classics, but ended up giving away the store. We were deep in the red, so I thought I'd save some money." His bark of laughter rang with bitterness. "I laid off Margaret and replaced her with a bookkeeping service. The new guy keeping Classics' books was skimming, and by the time I realized it, he'd skipped town."

Out of the corner of his eye, Cooper could see Paige hovering a polite distance away. He turned away from her.

"None of the banks would lend me money," Nathan continued.

"Did you go to Dad?"

"No!"

Cooper didn't blame his brother for not considering that avenue.

"I got desperate, and...I borrowed from the wrong people."

Something in Nathan's voice triggered an alarm. "And?"

"They play rough."

Cooper straightened instantly. "Are you all right? They haven't—"

"Not yet. But they're looking for me."

"What about the bookkeeper? Did you go to the police?"

"Me and about twenty other pigeons, but he's in Brazil. Probably living in a villa by the sea that he bought with our money."

"What money?" Cooper snapped. "Sounds to me like after you finished with Classics there wasn't anything left for him to steal!"

"To hell with you!"

"Damn it, Nathan—" Realizing his temper was taking control, and that his brother had done the best he could, Cooper stopped the recrimination poised on his tongue. With impotent fury, he plowed his fingers through his hair.

Nathan remained silent, possibly struggling with his own frustration and worry.

"Are you in danger?" Cooper finally managed in a quieter tone.

The younger man released a sharp sigh. "I'm safe enough for now."

"Together we'll handle this one step at a time, Nathe. The first and most important thing is to guarantee your safety. What will it take?"

Nathan told him the sum.

It was more than they could easily handle, but less than Cooper had feared. And Nathan was in danger. "If you sold the equipment—" he drew a fortifying breath and plunged, his gut twisting "—the cars, and the inventory of parts, that should cover most of what you owe."

"God, Coop, if I sell the equipment and inventory, Classics is dead!"

"Just *do* it. How do your accounts receivable stand? If you can collect at least half of what's owed you will that be enough?"

For a moment Nathan didn't answer. Then, "That will take care of it. But there won't be anything left of the business."

Cooper lifted his face to stare up at yellowed ceiling tiles. He felt as if he'd been gored. "I know."

"Coop, what can I say?" Nathan demanded raggedly. "I know how much you love that company—"

"I can start another company. Brothers are harder to come by."

"I . . . Thanks."

"I'll see you when I get there."

After he hung up the receiver, Cooper reluctantly turned to face Paige, afraid he'd see pity. But in her beautiful eyes he found only concern. At that moment he badly wanted to draw her into his arms and just hold her, resting his cheek on the top of her blond head, taking comfort in her presence.

They each had their problems. His brother and their business. Her stricken elderly cousin.

He knew Paige needed comfort, too, but she refused to take it from him. So he would not reach for her.

As he brushed by her in the narrow hall, heading toward the restaurant exit, he glimpsed the question in her eyes.

She followed without comment.

As they walked side by side across the parking lot, Paige finally broke the silence. "Let's take a chance on the old radiator. If we're careful, maybe it will get us to Florida. Then you can catch a flight out of Orlando, to Jacksonville."

With what? he thought bitterly.

As if reading his mind, she continued, "I'll pay your airfare as my portion of the trip."

Cooper scowled. "The deal was—"

"The deal was I'd finance the trip if you'd keep the car running. But you're doing both. I mean, we probably could have made it with my money, but we'd have been sleeping in the car and—"

"No."

They reached the car and she stopped, turning to face him. "Yes." Her blue eyes flashed. Her mouth formed a stubborn line.

That sexy, soft, delectable mouth.

Cooper felt his body tighten with desire. It was crazy, illogical! He knew that, but it still took the force of his will to resist pressing her against the car and exploring ways to bring the corners of that sweet mouth back up. He stood where he was, feet planted apart, hands clenching and unclenching at his sides.

And then he saw it. The shifting emotions in the depths of her eyes, her mouth softening.

"Don't look at me like that," he growled. "I'm a marine, remember?"

She drew a jagged breath. "Cooper, please..." Her voice held a pleading note.

What does she want from me? he thought savagely. *Understanding?* At that moment he didn't feel understanding. He felt angry. Frustrated. Hurt. And knowing she was capable of hurting him made him even angrier.

He pried his gaze from her face, and looked over her head. Congested morning traffic rumbled on the street, making its way to the parking lots of office buildings towering beyond. Mountains rose in the distance to surround the city on three sides.

"Get in the car," he told her flatly. "We have to go grocery shopping before we get back on I-10."

She didn't argue.

The ordeal at the grocery store wasn't as bad as he'd anticipated. Maybe he was just getting used to it. They bought their provisions and left without being stopped for smuggling in a rodent.

Once on the interstate, Cooper stayed in the slow lane, keeping his speed down to a nerve-gnawing, forty-five miles an hour. This was just something else he'd have to get used to.

As they drove east from Tucson, the grade gradually climbed. Cooper knew the car was laboring harder, so he took the precaution of pulling off the road every couple of hours. The third time they stopped, Paige made sandwiches. As he surveyed possible problem areas beneath the car's hood, she handed him a ham on rye and a cup of grape drink.

"How does it look?" she asked.

He concealed his surprise. Few words had passed between them since they'd left the restaurant that morning. Now it was one o'clock.

"The radiator hoses look bad. When we get to Lordsburg I'll replace them. The heater hose, too." He glanced at her as he took a bite of his sandwich.

She kept her gaze to oil-darkened machinery. "Okay. How long do you think it will take to make the change?"

He shrugged. "Couple of hours."

Paige fretted. A couple of hours for the hoses. An hour here and an hour there for the car to cool down. Creeping along at the minimum speed limit. Would they ever get to Plymouth? She'd counted on getting there with two weeks to spare before the tax auction. Now it looked closer to one. She spread the map over the front fender, tracing their route with a short-nailed finger.

"We should be able to make El Paso for the night, don't you think?" she asked.

Cooper popped the last bit of sandwich into his mouth and slammed closed the car hood. "Yeah. For the night."

Chapter Eight

Paige listened to the bathroom door of their small motel room close behind Cooper. She breathed a small sigh of relief, though she wasn't sure why she felt so relieved.

Yes she did. She knew exactly what was making her nervous.

Cooper.

He'd been so...so...*civil* to her today. But it hadn't taken her long to realize his politeness was a stick he used to keep her at a distance. Paige ruthlessly scrubbed her clean damp hair with the towel, then sat down, adjusted her robe, and set about combing out tangles.

She wanted the other Cooper back, the one who argued with her and desired her. The one who cared about her.

But she'd chased him away and she wasn't sure she could ever get him back. She wasn't sure it would be smart to try. She wasn't sure of anything anymore.

Tears gathered in her throat and she fought them, swallowing hard. Crying would get her nowhere.

Abruptly she stood and crossed the room to Henry's cage. She would hold him, pet him, and perhaps feel a little better.

The cage was empty.

"Oh no!" Paige breathed, horrified. "Not now, Henry! Now is a bad time to go exploring."

Frantically she searched the room, closely checking the seal of the door and the window, examining each dark corner, peering under and behind furniture. She didn't hesitate to strip the beds of their covers, carefully feeling for a soft, warm, wriggling lump. Finally she stood in the middle of the devastated bedroom and admitted there was only one other place Henry could have escaped to.

The bathroom.

She knelt on the floor and inspected the clearance between door and floor. A hamster as resourceful as Henry could easily squeeze through that space.

Paige could hear the water in the shower running. Quietly she tried the door. It was locked.

She rose up on her knees and knocked on the door. "Cooper, Henry's escaped from his cage. I-is he in there?"

The only answer was the hiss of the shower.

Paige knocked again, harder. "Cooper," she called, "is Henry in the bathroom?" Again she received no response.

She imagined Henry, a plump ball of fur shivering on cold tile, and Cooper's unsuspecting heel descending on him.

It was too much. She was losing everything that she loved, and it was all her fault. She'd left Waldo alone; she hadn't been vigilant enough of the bookkeeping; she was leaning too heavily on frail Maggie. She was torturing Henry daily with desert heat. And she'd driven sexy, wonderful Cooper away with her sharp tongue. Her fault. All her fault.

Paige huddled on the floor and vented her anguish in great sobs that tore from her chest and shook her body. Hot tears slicked her cheeks.

Suddenly the bathroom door jerked open, and warm humidity flooded into the room. Something struck Paige's side and fell across her back. Through the haze of tears, Paige saw Cooper crash into the side of the bed, landing on the floor with a muffled grunt. His legs tangled with hers as he struggled into a sitting position. He reached for her.

"Paige, are you all right?" he demanded urgently. Worry etched the strong lines of his face as he frantically examined her arms, her shoulders, her head. "Sweetheart, *talk to me!*"

"Everything, Cooper," Paige whispered. She hiccuped. "Everything is wrong." Well, almost everything. Cooper was there, leaning close to her. She wiped at her tears with the back of her hand.

He caught her damp hand in his and kissed the smear of tears. "No, sweetheart, everything isn't wrong. It just looks that way now. We'll make it right again."

A drop of water plopped onto her nose, and Paige looked up to find Cooper's dripping hair, which clung to his forehead and temples in dark, curving tendrils. As she watched the tiny runnels of water trickle over the broad, high cheekbones of his wet face, down his wet neck, to broad, wet shoulders, it dawned on her he'd left the shower suddenly. Glistening jewels of moisture bedewed curly chest hair. Jeans, zipped but not buttoned. Bare feet.

She looked up. Her gaze collided with his.

He didn't move.

His dark gold eyes searched her face. Perhaps, she thought, he expected her to turn on him again. She had hurt him once before. Before she could speak, he threaded his fingers through her hair and drew her face gently to his.

Cooper took her mouth in a claiming kiss. His lips moved boldly on hers, calling forth a shimmering treasure of feeling. A helix of emotion and sensation expanded within her. She closed her eyes and slid her palms up his chest, to his shoulders, needing an anchor.

He lifted his head. With a small murmur of protest at the loss, Paige raised her hands to urge him back to her.

Cooper rolled to his side, partially covering her, bearing his weight on his elbows. He kissed her, open-mouthed, and it excited her. She opened to him, eager to learn the taste of him.

Restlessly her hands roamed over his smooth shoulders, up and down his back, his arms. But it wasn't enough, not nearly enough.

He whispered her name, over and over, as his mouth moved across her cheek, her jaw, her temple. His breath tingled in her ear, sending a delicious shiver through her body.

Her robe had fallen open and through thin cotton and supple denim, she felt the hot, hard power of him. Dizziness seized her, making her light-headed.

Cooper touched her breast, stroking her through the flimsy material of her gown, teasing her with his fingertips. Paige moaned and blindly sought his mouth for another deep kiss. Her restless body, filled with molten need, moved against his.

He went still. She opened her eyes.

The skin of his high cheekbones pulled taut. A tightness framed his mouth. "Paige?"

"Yes?" she murmured.

He swallowed, and she found herself admiring the movement of his strong male throat.

His breath huffed against her cheek. "Are you sure this is what you want?"

Cooper told himself only an idiot wouldn't press home his advantage. He'd wanted this since the day he'd met her. Now all he had to do was push up her gown and open his jeans. It would be good. God, so good.

He gritted his teeth against the urgency of his arousal. The moment of truth. He would have laughed if it didn't promise to be so painful. His fantasy lay here before him, beneath him—and it wasn't enough. Not anymore.

He wanted more than Paige's sweet, willing body.

He wanted her heart.

Through the thick haze of passion, Paige struggled to comprehend what was happening. She realized Cooper had placed an important decision in her hands, one that would affect them both, one she should have been conscious of all along. Would have been with any other man. But Cooper was special. With him she shared this sizzling sexual attraction.

No. It wasn't just sexual attraction anymore. It was more. Much more.

She loved him.

And with that love came a burden: responsibility.

When they reached Florida, they would go their separate ways. They had to. Cooper served the military. She intended never to bear the designation "military dependent."

There was no future for them.

She looked up, memorizing each beloved feature in his strong-planed face. She reached up and traced his broad cheekbones with her fingertips.

"Cooper, this wouldn't be right."

He hung his head, drawing in a deep breath and letting it out. "I couldn't think of anything more right."

She knew he wasn't arguing, but she felt the need to justify her decision. "When we get to Florida, we'll be going our separate ways."

He eased himself away from her and slowly stood up. He offered her his hand. She took it, coming to her feet.

"We lead very different lives," she insisted.

"Meaning, I'm a marine."

She shook her head. "Meaning, I'm a civilian, and I like it that way."

He frowned. "I wasn't—"

"—Proposing. I know. You told me that in California. And I'm still not into one-night stands—"

"—Or cheap flings." His frown deepened.

Paige tried to smile and failed. "Cooper, I just wouldn't be comfortable with an affair."

He looked at her for a long minute and she wished she could fathom his thoughts. He slipped his fingers into her hair and urged her to him.

"Cooper," she protested weakly, but offered no resistance.

He brushed his lips across hers once, twice, then settled into a deeply tender kiss that left Paige speechless.

"It's late. Go to bed," he said softly, then turned and went into the bathroom, quietly closing the door behind him.

Seconds later Paige heard the shower come on, followed by Cooper's muffled exclamation.

The cold water gradually helped to clear Cooper's head. Despite the misery of his body, he smiled.

Paige had responded to him like a firecracker to a detonator. She wanted him as much as he wanted her. But more importantly, she had feelings for him.

Hope surged within him.

Her regret had been clear as she'd spoken of going their separate ways. That look confirmed what he'd already begun to suspect. All those cups of cool lemonade while he worked on the car. The extra slices of meat or cheese on his sandwiches. Tucking the bedcovers around his shoulders when she'd get up in the night and thought he was asleep. Those and the many other gestures and glances that warmed his heart.

Paige cared for him, all right. But he wanted more than that. He wanted her to love him as he loved her. She was too rare, too special for him to settle for less.

He turned off the water and grabbed a towel from the rack.

She cared for him. That was a start. The rest was up to him.

Deep in the night, Paige stirred, and cuddled further into the warm, protective shelter that enfolded her. Nice. So nice. Safe.

Something nagged at her sleepy mind. What shelter?

She came awake to discover herself in Cooper's arms.

A glance told her he was lying on top of the covers, wearing his jeans. He curled along the back of her, spoon-fashion.

She softly rubbed her cheek against his chest and smiled. Stubborn man.

Gently she pulled away from him just far enough to allow her to reach the thin bedspread rumpled at the foot of the bed. She pulled the spread up over Cooper, tucking it around his broad shoulders. Then she lay back down.

He murmured in his sleep and dragged her back into his embrace.

Content, Paige closed her eyes.

Sunlight spilled through a crack between the drapes. Paige struggled to sit up.

A warm, beautifully muscled arm pulled her back down into the tangle of sheets with little effort.

"Mmmphf."

She stifled a chuckle. It was cruel to tease the morning-impaired, but temptation proved too much for her.

Still separated by a sheet and blanket, she snuggled closer to the solid form and whispered in his ear. "Fire."

One amber eye shot open to glare at her.

Paige tried to keep from laughing.

Suddenly, Cooper reared up out of the bedcovers, startling a delighted shriek from Paige. He grabbed her and rolled her under him in a hopeless tangle of bedcovers. He planted one hand firmly on either side of her.

"Harass me, will you, woman?" he growled. "I have ways of dealing with perkiness at this obscene hour!"

She couldn't help it. Her laughter bubbled out.

He scattered light kisses down the side of her throat. "You will suffer."

Paige closed her eyes, enjoying the feel of his lips. "Oh, stop, stop, you're killing me," she told him in a monotone meant to convey disbelief. It would have worked better without that slightly breathless quality.

Cooper slowed his kisses, allowed them to become more sensual.

"Oh, Cooper," Paige sighed, and he felt his heart expand.

Something skittered over his foot.

That didn't feel like Paige. It couldn't be Paige. She was bundled in layers of covers.

It skittered up his ankle.

Abruptly, Cooper pulled away from Paige, shifting his weight, throwing back the bedspread.

Unexpected pain pierced his ankle and he yelped, startled.

"Henry!" Paige shouted, and quickly reached out, but the hamster scampered.

Sharp teeth sank into his toe and Cooper snarled. Before he could grab the damned beast, Paige corralled the fur ball and scooped him away.

Swearing, Cooper made a swipe for Henry, trying to gain him from Paige, ready to kill.

"Cooper, no!" she exclaimed, darting from the bed. "He didn't mean to hurt you. He's just frightened!"

Cooper's only answer was a murderous growl as he advanced on her. Step by step, she backed across the room toward Henry's cage. Step by step, Cooper advanced on her, unwilling to forgive and forget.

When she reached the dresser, Paige whirled around, quickly placing Henry inside the relative safety of his cage. She turned to face Cooper.

"Now, Cooper. Honey. Calm down. He's just a tiny, little hamster," she reasoned hastily. "You scared him, that's all. He's so small, he couldn't really hurt you." She glanced down and saw Henry had drawn blood. "Well, it wasn't like he *wanted* to hurt you."

"That rodent hates me," Cooper said in a low even voice. "He has always hated me. He will *always* hate me. The feeling," he enunciated, glaring past Paige at the hamster, "is mutual. I think we should settle this now."

"You're six feet, three inches tall and a trained warrior. Henry weighs about eleven ounces and has four teeth. Not exactly a fair fight."

Cooper turned his glare on Paige. "Four teeth that you can see. He's probably got more. In fact, I'm sure he has."

She moved to Cooper and slid her arms seductively around his neck. "My poor baby," she crooned. "Let me kiss your wounds. Let me make them better."

He resisted, but Paige noted with satisfaction that it cost him effort.

"He's probably given me rabies," Cooper muttered. "I need coffee."

Two hours later, they were on Interstate 10. Breakfast had been purchased at the drive-through window of a fast-food place. Cooper had downed the first cup of coffee and polished off his meal before Paige had taken five bites. He took his time with the second cup of coffee, thinking about last night, about Paige. He leaned back against the passenger door, replete, then proceeded to fill his eyes with her.

Paige watched the road. "Please don't do that."

"Do what?" Cooper asked innocently.

"Stare at me. It makes me uncomfortable, and it's very rude." Her smile abolished any hope of his taking her words as a reprimand.

"Rude? Me? I'm never rude," he informed her with mock primness. "I'm an officer and a gentleman."

Quickly, Paige took a gulp of her drink, scalding her mouth.

Officer. He was an officer, a military officer, and she didn't want to think about it. She'd made her decision. He would be hers to love for the duration of this trip, but everything ended in Florida. Everything but the memories.

Paige knew beyond doubt that for the rest of her life she would be comparing men to Cooper. He would be her example of what a man should be. She refused to allow herself to wonder if anyone would ever measure up to him; there was too much room for doubt. It hurt to think of saying goodbye.

She refused to consider anything but the present. Here and now. For the next few days they'd continue to live in their own special world. It would have to be enough.

The hours passed as they moved steadily southeast from El Paso. The scenery was arid, monotonous, but it didn't matter. Their attention focused on each other.

Cooper related his conversation with Nathan to her and Paige felt badly about the fate of Cooper's business. Instinctively she sensed it was an important part of his life, and she viewed it as a key to better understanding him.

"I'm sorry about Classics, Cooper," she said hesitantly, unsure of his response to the subject.

He didn't speak for a moment. "So am I."

"Can it be salvaged, do you think?"

Cooper adjusted his hands on the steering wheel. "I doubt it. But I won't know until I get there."

"Did you and your brother start the company together?"

"No." He shot her a crooked smile. "I started it. It was just supposed to be a hobby, because I already had a career, but I kind of got sucked into it. One thing led to another. Everything was so interesting. So *challenging*. Creating a viable business." He sounded a little amazed. "You can start with something small and build on it." Cooper shook his head. "There are so many facets. *You* know what I mean. You have a business."

"It is exciting, isn't it? And a lot of hard work." This new animation in him fascinated Paige.

"Exactly! Hard work, but also smart work. You have to do your research, find that market. And when you do, and everything comes together—God, what a rush!"

"Why didn't you choose to go into business, Cooper?"

An unfamiliar expression crossed his face, then disappeared. He was quiet a second, then reached out and lightly stroked the line of her cheek with the back of his knuckles, and she moved closer to him. With the curve of his arm, he nudged her closer, settling her against him.

Paige noticed his failure to answer her question. With the pressure toward observing tradition, had Cooper realized he had a choice?

She breathed a small sigh and nestled closer to him.

"That's better," he murmured, pressing a soft kiss to the top of her head. "This is the way it should be."

"Mmm." If only it could be. Sadness swept over her, but she quickly banished it. They had so little time. She wouldn't waste it with foolish regrets.

Hot, Paige thought irritably. Everything was blazing, burning, bloody hot, and she was tired of it. She couldn't even lean against the car as they waited on the side of the road for the radiator to cool. The metal would sear her skin. She fanned her face with short, disgusted swipes of the map and squatted in the shade.

Cooper finished his cursory examination of the tread on the tires, and came to sit back on his heels beside her. "The left rear is nearly bald."

Paige vented a whiny sigh. "Great. Just great." Surprised at herself, embarrassed, she fanned faster.

Cooper smiled. "A little testy, are we?"

"No." She stared straight ahead. Sandy plain baked in the sun's shimmering blaze. Surely hell was landscaped just like this. Hair whipped away from her face, caught in the gale she created with her map.

He caught her busy hand in his, and she reluctantly looked up at him, feeling foolish.

"Okay," she agreed grudgingly. "So maybe I'm not little Mary Sunshine."

Gently he pried the map from her fingers, and tossed it into the car through the open door. "Are you one of those people who have to have their twelve hours sleep or they're no good to anyone? I guess morning people have their weaknesses after all," he teased.

"Eight," she corrected. "I only need eight hours sleep."

His smile grew. "Didn't get your full eight hours, last night, sweetheart?"

"No."

"Do you wish you had?" The smile was gone now. In the depths of his golden eyes she glimpsed a tumult of emotion.

She touched his cheek and found a trace of afternoon stubble. "No." And she knew it to be true. She couldn't be sorry, not with Cooper. Her only sorrow was the life ahead of her without him.

It was late when they pulled into the Tumbleweed Motel on the outskirts of San Antonio. Cooper checked them in, then drove around to park in one of the spaces in front of their room. He turned off the car's ignition and turned to Paige.

"Wake up, sleepyhead," he said softly, filled with warm affection.

She opened her eyes and straightened in her seat. "I'm awake."

"Mmm-hmm." He brushed a stray lock of hair from her cheek. "You go on and take your shower. I'll unload the car and be right in."

"I can help," she protested.

"It will only take me a minute." Cooper pressed his lips to her forehead. "Go."

He went before her, unlocking the room and checking it, flicking on the lights.

"Cooper," she murmured as they passed. She lifted her face up for his kiss.

Instead of giving her a quick kiss, he stopped. Avoiding the hamster's cage she carried, he took her in his arms and eagerly slanted his mouth across hers.

Paige's body responded to his touch, filling with a heavy, needful ache.

He raised his head. "Go on," he said, his voice husky. "I'll be finished unloading in a minute."

After settling Henry for the night, Paige walked into the bathroom. It was little bigger than a closet. The shower stall—there was no bathtub—was about the size of a telephone booth.

She reached in and turned on the water, then stripped off her clothes. Picking up her shampoo and conditioner, she stepped into the spray. As she lathered the green liquid into her hair, a clean, herbal scent filled the shower.

Would Cooper come to her bed again and hold her through the night? Although his nearness vibrated her nerve endings, Paige enjoyed the feeling of closeness, of intimacy. The sight of Cooper asleep, his face relaxed, his hair tousled. The sound of him, that soft sush of his deep, rhythmic breathing. The feel of him, muscular, long-limbed, and solid. She treasured each precious aspect.

Each memory would count. In a few days, it would be all she had left of Cooper.

Chapter Nine

On this moonless night, only the bright halo cast under the musty curtain by walkway lights illuminated the room. Under the small window, the ancient air conditioner hummed. At a time when everything in her life seemed to be changing, Paige found reassurance in the familiarity of the sound.

As she lay curled against Cooper, separated by layers of covers, she felt attuned to him as never before. Yet a restlessness filled her. She resisted the urge to shift, afraid her movement might wake him.

"You awake?" Cooper asked quietly.

"Yes."

"No major mishaps today," he observed.

"No."

"Last night you called my name in your sleep."

She turned in his arms, to see his face. "I did?"

"You did."

"I don't remember a dream or anything."

He grinned. "It's those 'or anythings' that will get you every time. Must be deep-seated or maybe even repressed."

Paige didn't know why, she just knew she wanted to speak his name now. "Cooper," she whispered. "Cooper Angelsmith." The act of saying it gave her a peculiar, fundamental satisfaction.

"Yes." Longing rode his voice. "You make my name special."

"*You're* special."

He levered himself up on an elbow, and regarded her for a moment from shadowed eyes. She tried to fathom his thoughts but his features revealed no clue. Then he leaned down to feather his parted lips over her forehead, her eyelids, her cheeks. He slanted his mouth over hers in a slow, sweet kiss that spoke eloquently of trust.

Then he met her gaze and said, "Paige, I love you."

Unexpectedly, anguish stabbed her. She had hoped for this moment, longed for it, but now, instead of feeling only the purity of happiness, she was seized in a coil of conflicting emotions. She drew slightly away from him to conceal the trembling of her lips, then buried her face against the side of his neck, hugging him to her in desperation.

Cooper was an honorable man—he'd proven that time and time again. She must be honorable, too. He deserved that.

As much as she wanted to, she could not tell him of her love. It wouldn't be right. It wouldn't be fair. He might make plans for a future they couldn't share.

What they had together must end with this journey.

Suddenly she realized how important that was to her— that he not forget their time together. Because she knew he'd live in her memory, in her dreams, for the rest of her days.

She would show Cooper she loved him. Paige clung to him, skimming her hands over his shoulders, down his strong arms, memorizing the texture of his skin, the contours of his body. Immediately he drew her closer into his embrace. She reached up to frame his face between her palms and covered his wonderful mouth in a fierce kiss.

Oh, yes. She would show him.

He finally eased away from her, tossing back the bedspread.

"Cooper?"

He headed toward the bathroom. "Go to sleep, sweetheart," he told her in a tight voice, then closed the door.

She heard the shower come on.

The next morning they managed to get an early start. After breakfast, they each went to one of the restaurant's telephones.

Paige dialed Maggie's number.

"They moved Waldo out of intensive care yesterday," Maggie said, her smile coming through the line loud and clear. "It's too early to call him now, but later you might try. He wants to hear from you. He's been worryin'."

The hour time difference between San Antonio and Plymouth made no difference with Maggie, always an early riser, but Paige realized that a call now would probably awaken Waldo.

"You tell him not to be concerned, Maggie." Paige glanced at Cooper, who was intent on his own call. "I've got a very reliable traveling partner."

"That fella who came on with you in California workin' out okay, eh?"

"You could say that."

"Oh?" Maternal interest flavored Maggie's question.

"He's wonderful, Maggie. I've never met anyone like him." And never would again.

The older woman chuckled. "Are you goin' to keep him?"

Paige swallowed hard. With effort, she dragged her answer up through a tightened throat. "No."

"Well, why on earth not?" Maggie demanded. "Good men don't grow on trees, girl."

"He's in the military."

Pause. "Oh."

"You know how I feel about that," Paige persisted defensively.

Maggie sighed. "This man of yours—"

"He's not *mine,* exactly. I mean, we haven't talked about marriage—"

"And you're not goin' to give him the chance, are you?"

"It would only make things worse. I don't want to…hurt him."

"Well, then, I guess what you feel for him isn't the real thing."

Paige scowled. "What do you mean, not the real thing?"

"If you loved him, you'd want to be with him always," Maggie said, as if any simpleton should know that.

"I do—" Paige caught the rise in her volume and started again in a lower voice. "I do want to be with him always. But it doesn't work that way when a man's in the military, especially the marines. He'd be gone half the time. I'd be left behind, waiting."

"Maybe he's worth waitin' for."

Paige found no words to counter that.

"You just think about it," Maggie continued, her voice now soft with sympathy.

Tears burned at the back of Paige's eyelids. She drew a long breath. "I've got to go now, Maggie. I'll call Waldo later."

She hung up the receiver and stood for a moment staring down at her scuffed leather sneakers. *Maybe he's worth waiting for.*

Finally she looked up to find Cooper still involved in his conversation. She left to order two cups of coffee to go.

By the time they'd crossed into Louisiana, the highway had taken them past rice farms and wooded marsh. Eventually dense forest grew up on either side of the road like dark ramparts.

Cooper barely noticed. He was busy learning about Paige, about her life, while sharing his with her.

He'd never have guessed how involved it was to develop new shades of orchids. Oh, he'd studied all that stuff about Mendel's peas in school, but this was real life. This was Paige. He shared in her excitement over her success in developing export markets. The quality and uniqueness of Enchanted Orchids' plants were now known in fifteen states and six foreign countries.

Waldo had encouraged her. She gave her elderly cousin more credit than Cooper thought he was probably due, more credit than Waldo would likely claim.

"You've really been through thick and thin together, haven't you?" Cooper mused.

Paige smiled, her bright blue eyes reflecting treasured recollections. "Yes. Waldo never let me quit. He wouldn't allow me to fall by the wayside and whine." Her smile faltered and disappeared. "Now that he needs me, he's all alone."

"No, he's not. You told me yourself, Maggie visits him every day. And they're about the same age, aren't they?"

"Yes."

"Well, that should keep things lively."

She chuckled. "Oh, yes. Those two are always sparring."

He grinned. "Sounds like love."

"Ha! They'd both probably fall down laughing if they heard that!"

"Really? Look how we started out."

She shifted in her seat. "You told me about what happened with Nathan, but you didn't say what you plan to do about Cooper's Classics now."

He noticed her change of subject but decided not to press. Maybe he was wrong, and Waldo and Maggie were just bickering. Or maybe Paige wasn't ready to accept the idea of a man-woman relationship between her cousin and her friend. Another idea occurred to him, one that made sense, considering their own situation: maybe she found it difficult to talk about love. Cooper smiled to himself. He'd help her past that hurdle.

"When I spoke with Nathan this morning, he said he'd managed to collect a nice hunk of the receivables owed. He's found buyers for all of the equipment and some of the inventory. He seems to think he has a good chance of wrapping everything up by the end of the week."

"Gee, three days—that doesn't give him much time."

Cooper still struggled with his anger over the situation. Nathan had screwed up—royally. Now Cooper's Classics was nothing but a dissected corpse. "No, it doesn't."

"Do you plan to start another company?"

"No."

"Why not? Before you got the bad news from Nathan you were always excited when you talked about your company. I've never seen you that enthusiastic when you've mentioned the Marine Corps."

A muscle jumped high in his cheek. "That's different," he said shortly.

"Really? How?"

He glanced away from the road to Paige's wide eyes, then back to the road. "Because Classics is a...a *hobby*. I chose the Corps as my career."

For several seconds they rode in silence. Cooper opened his hands on the steering wheel, then, one by one, curled his fingers back over the solid plastic.

"Okay," she said. "As long as you chose your career."

They drove into Baton Rouge a little after six in the evening. Someday, Paige thought wistfully, she'd like to come back and see more of the cities and towns they'd passed through than just grocery stores, motels, and twenty-four-hour restaurants. Here in Baton Rouge they'd also take in the ambience of a Laundromat.

First they located a modest little motel and checked in, leaving Henry and their luggage in air-conditioned comfort. Then Cooper dropped Paige and their dirty clothes off at a coin laundry and went in search of a case of oil for the car.

She claimed three machines, then opened the two plastic garbage bags and began sorting. The news of Waldo's heart attack had come the day before she usually did her wash, which had left her with few clean clothes and a bundle of dirty. Cooper had packed light, expecting to fly home. Too light, it had turned out.

She experienced a flutter as she dropped his sexy briefs— there was nothing regulation about Cooper's underwear— into the tub with her bras and panties. She told herself she was being silly. After all, she was sleeping with the man.

On this hot summer's night, as she sat in the flimsy plastic and metal-rod chair, watching the traffic on the street of this working-class neighborhood, Paige realized true intimacy between a man and a woman was more than sharing a kiss. It was also more than having sex. True intimacy was doing a man's laundry with your own so often it became *our* laundry. Duty, compromise, and faith comprised real intimacy. It was something that required time and patience and ... acceptance.

Maybe he's worth waiting for.

She knew Cooper was worth many sacrifices. Was waiting one of them? Could she endure the separations? The loneliness? So many women did.

One by one, lights indicating it was time to add the fabric softener came on, and Paige measured the creamy blue liquid into each load. As she shut the last lid she turned to consider the other patrons. How many of the woman here were military wives waiting for their husbands to return? Did they possess a strength of character she lacked? Or were they simply not as wise as she?

She released a deep sigh and leaned stiff-armed against the edge of the washer. When she thought of parting from Cooper forever, she didn't feel very wise.

Maybe she should take the chance and see where it led. Maybe the separations wouldn't be as bad as she thought. Maybe Cooper was worth anything.

Large, male hands slipped around her waist. *"Ah, ma petite chou,"* said a warmly familiar voice next to her ear. "Do you not love the Gallic charm of this establishment? It is like Paris in springtime, *non?"*

Laughing, she turned to face Cooper. *"Non* is right. I'm sure there are lots of places in Baton Rouge just loaded with Gallic charm, but this Laundromat isn't one of them."

He wiggled his eyebrows. "Then it is up to us to lend it that certain *magique*. 'Ow about a French kiss?"

She gave him a quick peck on the tip of his nose. He grumbled as she coaxed him over to the chair next to hers.

"The clothes are in spin-dry cycle now," she assured him.

"But they still have to be dried."

"Well, yes."

"What kind of soap did you use?" he asked.

She told him, and he shook his head. "That won't do at all. Not at *all*. What softener did you use? The pink kind or the blue kind?"

"The blue kind," she answered, frowning. Then she caught on. He was teasing her.

"No, no, no, *no*," he said with exaggerated officiousness. "Everyone knows the pink kind is the best. Less static cling. Don't you watch daytime television?"

"Merciful heavens! What have I been missing?"

Like toppled dominoes in a row, each machine stopped with a clunk, and Paige took the clothes from the machine on the end and transported them to a dryer, feeding in quarters. When she came back over to Cooper she discovered he'd opened a washer. In his hands were two items: a pair of European-style, midnight blue briefs, and a violet lace bra. He stared at them for a moment, then looked up to catch her gaze. Heat rose in her cheeks. He gave her a wicked smile.

"You let our underwear rub together in a public place?" he asked in a low voice meant only for her.

Embarrassed, and feeling foolish for it, she snatched her bra from him. "Toad!"

He caught her wrist in a gentle hold. "I like it," he told her. "I like sharing everyday things with you."

Paige studied his face. He was serious and so typically Cooper that it wrenched at her heart.

She slipped her wrist free and quickly gathered all the articles from the delicate wash, stuffing them into one of the plastic bags for drying later in the bathroom.

"Hey." A callused finger tipped her chin up, compelling her to look at Cooper. "I mean it. The way we've come to accept each other's idiosyncrasies, all the little common grounds we've discovered—these things are important."

She needed to be assured, and while that neediness irritated her, she gave in to it. "What idiosyncrasies?"

His smile told her he knew he'd scored a point, but she decided that was only fair. "Well, for one, the way you've come to say as little as possible to me in the morning, until I've finished my second cup of coffee."

"And a complete breakfast!"

His smile widened into a grin. "And breakfast." He gradually sobered. "I want us to learn all those funny little quirks. I like the thought of us one day being—"

"Intimate," she supplied, thoughtful.

He seemed to consider the word. "Intimate. Yes, that's what I want." He slipped his palm down her upper arm in a light caress. "I was awake last night when you drew the covers over me. I never thought something so simple could mean so much." He caught and held her gaze. "It's nice to have someone who gives a damn. A partner."

Emotion swelled in her chest. "We've been partners since we started out in California."

"No we weren't. We had a common goal—to get to the east coast—but we couldn't agree on anything else. Only gradually have we become partners."

Silence settled between them.

Finally he cleared his throat. "Guess we'd better get this last load into the dryer, huh?"

"Yes, and I need to find a phone. I'm going to try again to reach Waldo."

"There's a phone over there, on the other side of those big dryers. Go ahead. I'll take care of this."

As she wound her way between patrons, laundry baskets, and children, Paige thought she and Cooper might have a chance after all. With a light tread, she stepped up to the black pay phone.

The hospital routed the call through to Waldo's new room.

"How's my girl!" His usually robust voice was shockingly thin and reedy. Tears sprang to Paige's eyes.

"Missing you, Waldo. I wish I was there with you right now."

"I know you do, missy, I know you do. But soon you'll be home, and so will I. To celebrate I'll make my famous enchiladas."

"*In*famous, you mean. I have scar tissue on my tongue."

Waldo chuckled. "I never noticed you passing up a second helping."

Paige smiled. "I just didn't want to hurt your feelings."

"Ha!"

"Okay, okay. I *love* your enchiladas, I have *always* loved your enchiladas, I *will* always love your enchiladas. Even when you start using heart-sensible ingredients, which you're going to start using as soon as you start cooking again."

She could almost hear him turn his nose up. "Between you and Maggie, I'll probably wind up cooking godawful oatmeal," he grumbled.

Paige heard Maggie's voice say, "You stubborn old buzzard! We're just tryin' to keep you alive—though it's probably more trouble than it's worth."

Having been through thousands of these exchanges between her cousin and her friend, Paige knew right about now Waldo would be giving Maggie a rakish grin and a

canny wink, and that the older woman would blush furiously.

"When are you getting out of the hospital, Waldo?"
Paige asked.

"Soon as possible!"

"So they haven't given you a release date yet?"

"I keep trying to get one, but these doctors know a good
pin cushion when they have one. They don't want to let me
go. They're probably selling my blood on the black market. I've got a rare blood type, you know."

"Yes, Waldo, I know." Thank God for insurance. But
even their insurance wouldn't cover all the bills.

"Waldo, I don't like to bring this up now. . . ."

"Spit it out, missy. Does this have something to do with
that marine Maggie told me you're traveling with?"

"Uh, no. No, this is about our money, yours and mine.
Enchanted Orchids'."

"What about it?"

She shifted her weight from one sneakered foot to the
other. "Where is it, Waldo? I asked Maggie to find the
checkbook, and she couldn't. Which bank has our accounts? The property taxes are overdue."

"Property taxes? Overdue?"

"Where is our money?" she persisted in a soothing voice.

"Safe," he insisted. "Safer than it would be in any
bank."

A stone of dread dropped into the pit of her stomach.
"Waldo, please tell me where you've put our money."

"I buried it."

"Buried it," she echoed stupidly.

"That's right, I buried it. Missy, I saw it coming all over
again. Banks failing right and left! They got me the first
time, but I wasn't going to give them a chance to get me and
mine again."

She didn't want him to get excited. Nothing was worth him having another heart attack. Instead she said, "Then you paid the taxes. Right, Waldo?"

There was a pause. "I can't seem to recall."

"The county's saying the taxes are more than two years overdue."

"Don't you believe it! I'd never let something that important slip by! Scoundrels, that's what they are!"

His agitation alarmed Paige. "Okay, okay. No problem. Just tell me where you buried it. As soon as I get home, I'll dig up what I need." *All* of their money! Well, most of it. If he felt safer with something stashed away, then that's the way it would be.

"Can't do that."

Paige silently prayed for patience and understanding. "Why?"

"Someone might overhear. In a hospital, there's no such thing as privacy. I'll tell you when you get here. I know where every dime of it is."

"What about telling Maggie? Then she could go someplace private and call me."

"No. If I told Maggie she'd go get out her shovel and go digging so you wouldn't worry about those taxes. She's too old for that. She might hurt herself," he said firmly. There was an indignant squawk in the background. "You're younger and stronger," Waldo continued, unperturbed. "I'll tell you when you get here. Until then...well, the walls have ears."

"Gee, Waldo, just how much do we have? Are we talking about the Windsor fortune, here?"

"It doesn't take much to tempt people," Waldo said grimly. "I once saw a man murdered for a quarter and the shoes he had on his feet."

The Depression, Paige thought, with a sinking feeling. All this went back to his experiences in the Great Depression. No amount of coaxing on her part would change his mind, and his precarious health kept her from trying.

Waldo asked how things were with her, and she gave him an edited version of the trip from Tipilo. Then Paige wrung from him the promise that he'd obey the doctors. She gave Maggie the phone number of the motel and promised to call them the following day.

She breathed a sigh of relief as she replaced the receiver in its cradle. Waldo was out of intensive care. And he sounded in good spirits—an observation Maggie had confirmed. From here on out, Paige promised herself, it was low cholesterol and high fiber.

The taxes were another matter entirely. The only way to save her home and her business was to get back to Florida in time to learn the location of the money, then dig it up and pay the tax collector. Suddenly the time remaining— four days—didn't look like enough. But it had to be.

She chewed her lips as she walked around the corner of the large dryer. Luck had been with Cooper and her for the last two days. Maybe it would hold a few days longer. Once she dug up the money, she would pay for Cooper's airfare to Jacksonville. She'd said she would finance this trip, but he'd been paying most of the bills. Paige always kept her promises. Besides, maybe everything would work out. His money. Her money. Their money…

She looked across the room to see Cooper at a long table, folding their clean clothes.

A lovely, dark-eyed woman kept trying to help him, teasing him in a lilting voice, laughing merrily when he good-naturedly declined. Finally she gave up. She waved to him over her shoulder as she slowly sashayed over to the soft drink machine.

Other women in the Laundromat, Paige now noticed, flirted with their eyes, with their smiles—some shy, some brazen. And to all of them, Cooper was polite, even mildly gallant, but never did he appear to return their interest.

But what if he was married, and had been away from wife and home for months? Away from the things familiar to him. Uprooted. Lonely. Then how would he receive the flirtations of other women? Would he succumb? And would his wife, lying alone in her double bed, night after night, wonder? When she read his letters, would it occur to her that he might not be telling her everything he'd done? Would it trouble her?

It had troubled Paige's mother, though she'd never spoken of it directly. Paige could no longer recall how many times her father had gone to sea. Now it seemed he'd seldom been home. But she remembered the pale figure of her mother walking the dark halls of their house at night.

It would trouble Paige. She wanted a husband who would live at home with her, all year long, every year. One who would be with her to celebrate the holidays, birthdays, and anniversaries. She couldn't bear the thought of living as her mother too often had: married yet single, with all the obligations and few of the privileges of either state.

In Florida, Paige thought, her chest constricting in grief. She would say goodbye to Cooper in Florida.

Now she drank in the sight of him as he folded their clothes. He carefully folded each garment, then, realizing it looked more like he'd wadded and tossed, he shook it out and tried again.

Paige drew several ragged breaths. There would never be another Cooper in her life. But she'd have to learn to cope with her pain. She just couldn't live life as a military wife. And that was the only kind she'd have with a military man.

* * *

They returned to their room, and Paige quickly hung their underwear up in the bathroom. When she finished, the towel rods and the shower curtain rod were covered.

As she stood in the tiny doorway, staring at the rainbow of her lacy things mingling with the darker colors of Cooper's sexy briefs, he came up behind her.

"Sweetheart, what's wrong?" he asked softly. "Ever since you made that call to Waldo you've been quiet. Is he all right?" Gently he turned her around to face him. "What is it?"

He was too sensitive to her moods to try to fool him with a bright smile, Paige realized. And she was greedy enough to keep every moment she had left with him.

"Waldo is improving." She leaned into him, and his arms encircled her in an embrace that she'd come to associate with heaven. "The county claims no property taxes have been paid on our land for over two years, so in nine days it will be put up for auction. I've called the tax collector's office—Waldo is so conscientious about paying bills—but they show no record of payment."

"What about the canceled check?"

"There is no canceled check. Apparently Waldo has been using money orders for everything."

"Money orders? Why?" Cooper smoothed a stray tendril of hair from her forehead and pressed a kiss in its place.

"Because he never put our money in a bank. He buried it."

"What?" He drew away to scan her face, then quickly enfolded her again, hugging her.

After a moment's silence, he asked her, "Don't you have a personal checking account?"

She nodded, her cheek rubbing the front of his oxford cloth shirt. "Yes. Waldo was depositing a portion of my salary into it every two weeks. But he had his heart attack just before payday, and I was left with very little money. I didn't have enough money for a plane ticket. Arnold gave me that old car we're driving. Bless his heart, I know he thought it was in better shape than it is.''

"Why didn't you leave Henry with Arnold and take a bus?"

"He has three cats that are very good at killing birds and mice. Besides, Arnold doesn't like hamsters."

She could feel his lips curve against her hair. "Perfectly understandable."

"So that leaves me four days to get to Plymouth, to find out the location of the buried money from Waldo—who will only tell me in person—to dig up the money, and to pay the taxes."

"A lot to do in so little time," he agreed. "Why did Waldo bury the money?"

She explained about Waldo's experiences in the Depression and he listened quietly, continuing to hold her, there in the doorway.

Afterward he took her hand, led her over to the small table at the foot of the bed, and laid out the makings of their dinner.

"What would *mademoiselle* prefer? A turkey sandwich, or one, perhaps, of peanut butter and jam?"

Later, after they'd finished with dinner and each taken their showers, Cooper said, "I have something for you."

Paige looked at him, surprised. "Really?"

He reached under his pillow, then held up his closed fist. His fingers curled open. In the center of his palm rested a reddish brown stone in the shape of a rose. Attached to it was a small chain with a ring for keys.

"It isn't much," he said. "I wanted to buy diamonds or pearls, but I'm afraid the budget won't allow it. Still, I

wanted to get you something to remind you of this trip.''
Their eyes met. ''Whenever you use your keys, you'll think
of our adventure.''

Hesitantly she reached out and took the gift.

''The stone is called a desert rose,'' he told her.

She didn't try to stay the flow of tears. They slid un-
heeded down her cheeks and dropped onto the blanket that
covered her lap. ''A desert rose,'' she whispered, thinking
diamonds could never have meant as much to her as this
small brown rock.

''A flower in a hard land,'' he murmured. ''Like you.''
He reached out to brush away her tears. ''You're my desert rose.''

Later, when she drifted off to sleep, she was clutching her
key chain.

The sharp buzz of the telephone woke Paige, who bolted
into a sitting position. In the dark, she reached across
Cooper and groped around the bedside stand, finally
grasping the receiver. ''Hello,'' she rasped. What time was
it? It couldn't be morning yet.

''Paige,'' came Maggie's strained voice.

Immediately, Paige shot to full wakefulness. ''Maggie,
what's wrong?''

''Waldo's had another heart attack, and it's not lookin'
so good.'' Maggie drew a halting breath. ''We may lose him
this time, girl.''

Chapter Ten

Paige gripped the handset. "When did it happen? He's not suffering, is he?"

"Happened not an hour ago. He's sleepin' now. Doctors...th-they got him all doped up." Maggie finally broke down and sobbed.

Anxiety and frustration raged through Paige. She should be *there*, with Waldo. With Maggie. Instead she was meandering through Louisiana, selfishly enjoying her time with Cooper.

"I'll be there as soon as I can, Maggie." She wanted to say it would take only an hour, or even a day, but she couldn't promise two days and be certain of making it. God, she hated cars!

"Just take care, girl. You can't do anything for Waldo right now. I know you're tryin'."

As soon as they said good-night, Paige hung up and scrambled from the bed. Cooper, who'd awakened at the beginning of the conversation, watched her run into the bathroom and come out with her arms full of underwear.

"What are you doing?" He flipped back the bedspread and strode across the room to where she was throwing her belongings into her suitcase.

"I've got to go! We've got to leave *now,* this minute. I can't afford any more time!"

As she drew her arms back to hurl a brush onto the tumbled heap in the case, Cooper caught her wrist in gentle fingers. "What's wrong with Waldo, Paige?"

She stared at his hand as if she didn't see it. "He's had another attack. Maggie was crying." Her throat worked a moment, then she turned wide, frightened eyes up to him. "Maggie never cries."

He coaxed Paige into his arms. He could feel her tremble, and her hands were cold. "All right. We'll leave now. You take care of things here and I'll go check us out and fill the tank with gas, okay?"

She nodded, her cheek pressed to his chest. Slowly she lifted her head. "Cooper..."

"Yes, sweetheart?"

She studied his face, as if committing its every plane and texture to memory. "Nothing. Just...thank you."

He smiled and leaned down to kiss her tenderly. "My pleasure."

It didn't take long for Cooper to dress, check out, and gas up the car.

Muscles tense, he stepped into the phone booth in the parking lot of the filling station. He reached into his back pocket and slowly took out his wallet. From it he withdrew a slip of paper bearing an address and phone number. A muscle jumped in his jaw, and he realized his teeth were gritted. He released a harsh sigh, and tried to relax. Then he dialed the number and deposited the exact amount of change dictated by the operator.

A few minutes and connections later, a familiar voice answered.

Cooper thought of Paige, of her grief and her fear.

"Hello, Dad. I need your help."

"Are you sure you're not lost?" Paige frowned. "I don't remember it taking this long to get from the interstate to the motel."

Cooper continued to watch the road. "I know where I'm going."

A few minutes later they entered the airport.

"What are we doing here? Please, Cooper, we don't have time to waste."

He pulled alongside the curb at the Delta Airlines section and got out. Paige climbed out of the car and slowly walked back to where he was unloading her suitcase from the trunk.

"Cooper?"

He knew he was taking a risk. Maybe he was a fool, letting her out of his sight before things between them were settled. What if she wasn't sure she loved him yet? What if he was giving up his opportunity to convince her before she returned to her home turf?

If she didn't go now, she might lose her home turf. She might lose her time with Waldo. But she would never lose him.

He turned to her. "There's a ticket to Orlando waiting for you at the Delta counter. I'd go in with you but I can't leave the car here."

"How—?"

"I called Dad."

"But—"

"Don't worry about it, okay? Just…get on that plane."
He reached out and picked an invisible piece of lint off her
blouse. His voice softened. "Be there for Waldo and Maggie. Straighten out that mess with your taxes. I'll catch up
with you in the car." He cleared his throat. "And I'll take
the rat. *Henry*," he conceded.

Large, sky blue eyes filled with tears. "Oh, Cooper." She
flung herself into his arms.

He gripped her in a desperate embrace. How could he let
her go? It would be like losing his heart, his soul.

Finally he released her. "Go," he said hoarsely. "You
don't want to miss your flight." He gave her a lingering
kiss, then took a step back. "Give my best to Waldo and
Maggie. I'll see you in a few days."

Paige watched the car until it was out of sight, then
picked up her suitcase and went inside to stand in line. As
she slowly inched her way toward the counter, there was a
painful ache in the emptiness where her heart had been.

I'll see you in a few days.

By then, everything would have changed. Their journey
together had ended.

Anxious, weary, Paige stepped off the tram from the gate
concourse and walked out into the main terminal of Orlando International Airport.

Immediately, Maggie rushed forward from the crowd
waiting to meet arriving passengers, her arms opened wide.
"Paige!"

Paige dropped her tote. She hugged the older woman
firmly, needing that familiar comfort. "I missed you so
much," she said. "I don't know what I would have done if
you hadn't been here to take care of Waldo."

Maggie patted Paige's cheek with a weathered hand. "Well, you're home now. That's all that matters." Her brown eyes glistened.

Paige shouldered her tote as they headed toward the baggage claim area. "How is he? When I called you from the airport in Baton Rouge you said things weren't as bad as feared."

"He's an amazin' man, your cousin. Amazin'. He just refuses to stay down. He's already been taken off the machines. True, he's havin' a few little troubles, but that's to be expected. Doctors say therapy and time should take care of them."

They stepped off the escalator and went over to the appropriate carousel.

"He's goin' to fuss, but it's time for him to retire," Maggie said firmly.

Guilt shot through Paige. "I know. I should have refused to let him work so hard. Enchanted Orchids is my concern, not his."

"Hogwash. You could have talked till you were blue in the face, and old Mr. Know-It-All would've done exactly what he wanted—and that was to work. I know you've tried to get him to slow down. That man refuses to listen to reason. Stubborn old coot."

Tiredly, Paige smothered a grin. She spotted her scuffed suitcase and heaved it off the conveyer belt. "But he's doing well now, right?" she asked as she dug the strap out of her purse and clipped it to the case.

Maggie smiled. "Right."

They took the elevator up and stepped out into the parking garage, suitcase rumbling along in tow.

"That was mighty nice of your marine to get you a plane ticket," Maggie said.

Paige sighed, wondering if the hollow ache would ease with the passing of time, or if she was doomed to live with it always. "Yes. Yes, it was." She could guess what it must have cost Cooper to call his father for help. And he had paid that price for her sake.

"You say he'll be here in a few days?"

She was dreading that—the second parting. Yet mingled with that dread was the impatient anticipation of seeing him again. "That's right."

They arrived at Maggie's ancient pickup truck. Paige hoisted her case into the back and automatically reached to take the keys from her friend.

Maggie resisted. "You've been drivin' for days."

"You hate driving in Orlando traffic, and I don't mind. Besides, this jalopy will be a pleasure after fighting with that behemoth of mine for two thousand miles." She accepted the keys, then climbed into the cab. The truck started immediately. Waldo kept it in good running order, just as he did their own vehicles.

As they headed out of the airport, up Highway 436, Maggie brought her up-to-date with Waldo and Enchanted Orchids. She'd visited Waldo every day at the hospital. Sam, Paige's full-time help, and Maggie had kept the operations of Enchanted Orchids going, with the help of a neighbor's son, Joe. But no bills or salaries had been paid....

"It's a good thing I got here when I did," Paige said as she turned the truck into the hospital parking lot. "If I'd been gone much longer you would've ended up in the hospital, too."

Luck was with her and she found a parking place immediately. Turning off the ignition, she turned to Maggie. "What would Waldo and I ever do without you?" She leaned over and kissed her friend's weathered cheek.

Maggie squeezed Paige's hand lightly. "What would I do without you and Waldo?"

Fifteen minutes later they entered his room. The television was on, and in the far bed a middle-aged man watched the early morning news.

Waldo lay still and pale, his eyes closed. He looked so frail, Paige thought, emotion clogging her throat. So...old. A month ago he'd seemed the picture of energetic health.

She whispered his name, unwilling to disturb him if he was sleeping.

His eyes opened. "Paige?" he asked in a gravelly voice. Faded blue eyes focused. "Paige."

Tears threatened as she gently hugged him. "What am I going to do with you?" she scolded. "Always getting into trouble."

Waldo smiled faintly. "That's what happens when you leave me, missy. I just fall to pieces." He managed a wink.

She brushed a wisp of silver hair away from his high forehead. "I guess I just won't leave again. You can't be trusted to stay well."

"Stop fussing over me. Everything is all right. I'll be out of here in a few days, and then just try to keep up with me."

"Oh, no you don't!" Paige declared. "We're both going to exercise some good judgment for once. Enchanted Orchids has grown. It's too big an operation for just three people to run. Maggie says Joe has been a big help to her and Sam so I'm going to offer him a job."

"Joe's just a kid. What does he know about running a nursery?"

"He's not going to run the nursery. He's going to help. Maggie says he's smart and learns fast."

Waldo continued to frown.

"He could use the money for college, and we can use his help. Face it, Waldo, we did something right and the business has prospered."

"Is this the brush-off?" her cousin demanded. "The old man is past it, so put him out to pasture?"

Paige's scowl matched her cousin's. "Be glad you're under a doctor's care, Waldo, because if you weren't I'd smack you!"

"No self-respectin' pasture would have you, you old buzzard," Maggie stated.

"Oh, is that so?"

Maggie nodded. "Yep. A lot of real interestin' things go on out in those fields. *Real* interestin'. But you'd miss it all because you'd be out there mopin' and feelin' sorry for yourself. You'd sink so far down in self-pity you'd be no good to anyone." She turned to Paige. "Did I tell you that I'd signed up for the substitute grandparent program at the elementary school?"

Paige vowed that if Maggie ever needed a cheering section, she'd volunteer in a heartbeat. "No, you didn't. How do you like it?"

"Haven't started yet. Orientation is in two weeks. Do you know, some of those youngsters have never been around a senior? Many of them have never even met their own grandparents."

"Oh, Maggie, how sad."

Waldo made a face. " 'Oh, Maggie, how sad,' " he mimicked in falsetto, then groused in his normal voice, "Have I suddenly faded into the woodwork? I want an answer. Am I being retired?" He fixed Paige with a stern look.

"It will depend on your health. You're precious to me, Waldo. I won't endanger you."

"You're going to take the doctor's advice, I suppose," he accused. "As if he knew anything. They're all just *practicing* medicine. Maybe someday one of them will get it right."

Noticing his increasing pallor, Paige kissed his forehead and pressed him back until he rested against the elevated bed. She offered him a sip from his glass of water, trying to think of a way to broach the subject of the buried money without exciting him.

"We need to talk about the taxes, Waldo."

He nodded tiredly.

"Do you remember paying the property taxes in the past two years? Do you have the validated receipts?"

Waldo blinked. "I... don't remember. I can't remember seeing a bill." He grasped her hand. "What are you saying, missy?"

Paige tried to smile reassuringly as she repeated what she'd told him yesterday. "The county says our taxes haven't been paid." She gave his hand a little squeeze. "But that's okay. We've got the money, right?"

"Right," Waldo affirmed.

"There's no problem then. Just tell me where you put the map. I'll go dig up the money and pay the county."

"There is no map. It's all in here." Waldo confidently tapped his temple with a forefinger.

"Oh. Well. Okay, tell me the location."

"I didn't hide it all in one place. The money is in several different spots—for safety's sake."

"Of course. I understand. Now tell me, Waldo, where—did—you—bury—it?"

He frowned in concentration. "Let's see now...." Slowly a blank expression stole over his face, followed closely by one of horror. "I don't know. I can't remember where I hid the money."

* * *

Cooper missed her. Without Paige, the drive was lonely and boring. He suspected that after having spent days with her verbal jousting and her sweet care, life would be dull. Too dull.

"What do you think, fella? Do you miss her, too?" Cooper glanced down at Henry, whose cage sat next to him on the seat, secured by the seat belt.

Henry uncurled and waddled over to the side of his cage, fixing his bright, black, beadlike eyes on the driver.

"Yeah, I thought you would," Cooper agreed. "She's something special, isn't she? And she loves me. That's become clear." He caught himself. Talking to a rodent. Worse—carrying on a conversation with a rodent. Boy, he must have really gone around the bend.

He glanced again at the hamster, who regarded him steadily. "I wonder if you and I could ever get along. I mean, on a permanent basis."

The small animal reared up on its hind legs and grasped the bars of the cage in its minuscule front paws.

Cooper nodded, looking back at the road. "I know, I know. It's a crazy idea. But...I love her, Henry. And I don't want to lose her. You're a bachelor. You know what it's like. The independence is great. But it's not as great as being with Paige."

Henry licked his paws and briskly groomed one ear.

"Believe me, Henry, you'd feel differently about the whole thing if you had a Paige of your own. Of the hamster persuasion, that is. No," Cooper concluded, "I've made up my mind. When we get to Plymouth, I'm going to ask Paige to marry me."

"It's got to be here somewhere." Paige tossed down the shovel and, grabbing the rag that dangled from her rear pocket, wiped her face. Grit rasped across her cheeks.

"Here's your water." Scowling, Maggie held out a large yellow plastic glass. Ice cubes clunked against the sides. "I don't know why you won't let me help you."

"Maggie, Waldo is right. This is heavy, nasty work. It's too hot and too strenuous for you to be out here digging in the dirt. If this was what he did every time he made a deposit, it's no wonder he had a heart attack. Besides, you *are* helping." Paige drank deeply. "Mmm. Thanks." She took another long swallow and handed the glass back.

They surveyed the landscape before them. A modest, thirty-year-old house. Five greenhouses. Oak trees. Pine trees. Old azalea bushes. And holes. Twelve large, fresh holes.

"If I were Waldo, where would I bury money?" Paige murmured. *"Where?"*

Maggie shook her head. "I wish I knew. Waldo wishes he knew."

Paige resettled her battered straw garden hat on her head and picked up the shovel. "Well, I don't want him worrying about it now. There's plenty of time for him to fret about it later, just before I wring his neck."

The older woman turned a stern gaze on Paige.

"Just kidding, Maggie. Sort'a. Go inside to the air-conditioning. It's too hot out here."

"I've lived here all my life, girl, and I'm well aware of what Florida's summer heat can do to a body. But it hasn't stopped me yet."

"Please, Maggie," Paige said softly.

"All right." She reached up to position a warning fore-finger in front of Paige's nose. "Just you remember, old women aren't the only ones who can get heatstroke. You take a break soon and come inside. I'll make some fresh iced tea for you.''

After Maggie disappeared into the house, Paige walked to the corner of the closest greenhouse and looked around for loose soil or disturbed foliage. There was usually a lot of activity in this area. Would Waldo have considered that a plus or a minus? She thought about it a moment, then released a frustrated sigh. Slowly she combed the area, studying the ground. She found no signs. Nothing to go by.

Her frustration tipped over into anger and she slammed the blade of her shovel into the earth near a stand of pines.

No one was going to take her home from her.

She flipped aside a clump of dirt, and slammed again.

No one was going to take her orchid houses from her.

The pile of sandy soil grew. *Slam.*

And damned sure, she vowed, her fury building, no one was going to take everything she'd earned for the mere price of back taxes!

Cooper stared at what lay before him. Once semi-pristine acres of central Florida had been ravaged by something large and molelike. Probably a herd of them, judging from the number of holes.

He glimpsed movement from the corner of his eye and turned to see Paige sitting several yards away in the shade of a maple tree, fanning herself with a straw hat. He grinned and strode toward her.

Paige saw him before he reached her. She'd dreaded this moment. Afraid it would hurt her to see him again, afraid she would hurt him, certain there would be pain when they parted. Suddenly all that was forgotten in the joy that rushed through her.

''Cooper!'' She flung herself into his arms as they met halfway.

He showered her upturned face with kisses, heedless of the smudges of dirt and grit. "Ah, sweetheart, no one has ever looked so good to me. I missed you."

"I missed you, too." She laughed. "I can't believe it's been less than two full days since you took me to the airport. It's seems so much longer."

"It seems like an eternity," he murmured, then slanted his mouth over hers. His strong fingers cupped the back of her head. Automatically their bodies fitted together.

Through the fabric of their jeans Paige could feel the steel of his thighs, and under her palms his powerful shoulders moved. Some elemental aspect rose in her to glory in his strength. Cooper was a man who could and would protect his own.

Her thoughts evaporated as he deepened the kiss.

Finally he lifted his head. A satisfied male smile curved his lips. "Yes, I can see you did miss me."

Paige lowered her lashes in what she hoped was a sultry look. "Is that a gun in your pocket...?"

"No." His smile grew into a grin. "I'm just mighty happy to see you."

"Mmm. *Mighty* happy."

With the tips of his fingers, he traced the streaks of grime on her cheeks. "Mind telling me what's going on? What's with the holes?"

"Waldo can't remember where he buried the money."

"He can't remember.... Didn't he write it down? Make a map?" Cooper asked incredulously.

She sighed, surveying her day's handiwork. "If he did, he can't remember."

"So you've been looking for your savings the hard way," he concluded.

"Under the circumstances, do you know an easier way?"

He considered her question for a moment. "No. Afraid not."

"Well, so far I've found two thousand dollars—enough cash to pay a little more than half the money owed. With our agricultural exemption, the taxes would have been a fraction of that, but Waldo didn't get around to filing for it this year. I guess the job was just getting to be too much for him." And now she had two days to find the rest of the money and to get it to the tax office. Two days.

"And you have absolutely no idea where Waldo might have hidden the rest?"

She swept an arm across the view before them. "He seems to have had a preference for mayonnaise jars."

He gazed out over the five acres that made up her property. "Mayonnaise jars."

Paige tried to memorize every detail about Cooper. She sharply regretted that she didn't have a picture of him. But she had no doubt she would remember the important things. His thoughtfulness. His laughter. His love.

It was time for her to let him go. He had problems of his own to straighten out.

By now she'd hoped to have his airfare unearthed, but she couldn't even offer him that. He could take the car. It wasn't what she wanted for him, but it was all she had.

"Let's get to work," he said. "If you've only got two days to find that money, every minute will count."

"What?"

"A shovel, please. I refuse to dig with my bare hands."

"Cooper—"

He set a finger firmly across her lips. "You need help, Paige. I know you wouldn't ask. So I'm offering. My business is gone, but there's still time to save yours."

He was right. She needed help. Desperately. But he might be expecting something from her she couldn't bring herself to give. And she couldn't stand the thought of using him. Or of him thinking she had.

He strode to where she'd left the shovel, and picked it up.

"No, Cooper, wait!" She sprinted the distance between them. "Listen to me—"

"Do you want my help or not?" he demanded.

Two days.

Paige released a harsh sigh. She felt as if she was selling her soul for the price of her home. Her home and Waldo's. "Yes. I want your help."

At noon Maggie bullied them into the house for the lunch she'd prepared. They took their shoes off at the door and padded into the kitchen in their socks.

Though working in the summer heat usually depressed Paige's appetite, Cooper polished off peanut butter and honey sandwiches and half a bag of potato chips. He ate with such relish she doubted he'd stopped for breakfast this morning.

"How much do you have left to go?" Maggie asked. "You've found almost enough, haven't you?"

Paige nodded as she swallowed a mouthful of iced tea. "Just two hundred, forty-seven dollars and thirty-six cents to go, then we'll be in the clear." She glanced around the room. "Where's Henry?"

"In your bedroom," Maggie answered. "Cooper brought him into the house immediately." Her eyes twinkled with amusement. "Hamsters are *very* susceptible to heat, you know."

Paige stared at Cooper in surprise.

He suddenly seemed to find the potato chip crumbs on his plate uniquely interesting. As he pushed them around with the tip of his finger, red crept up his neck to stain his face. "I, uh . . . well, it seemed pointless to drag the rodent this far only to let it die."

Paige resisted the urge to tease him. Instead she just grinned. "So true. And I'm sure you were careful only because you know how attached I am to him."

"Yes," Cooper agreed instantly. "That's it, exactly." He stood. "Well, time's a wastin'. We'd better get back to work if we're ever going to find that money." He turned to Maggie. "Thank you for fixing that delicious lunch, ma'am."

Taking her cue, Paige rose, too, and thanked her friend for preparing the meal. The women shared an instant of silent laughter before Paige trailed after Cooper.

As soon as the door closed behind them, he pulled her into his arms. There against the side of the house, he kissed her deeply. He seared his heat and need into every atom of her body until, if she'd still possessed a soul to trade, she would have given it to have him.

Straightening, Cooper drew a deep breath and released it. "For two days I've been missing you," he said, his voice rough with arousal. "I've missed your voice, your scent, the sight of you." He grinned lopsidedly. "I even missed your chatter at breakfast." His fingers wrapped around her ponytail and tilted her face to a more advantageous angle. He moved his mouth over hers with exquisite tenderness that pierced her heart with a dagger's blade.

"I love you, Paige."

She swallowed hard against the emotion that surged through her.

All she'd wanted was to love him. To enjoy his humor, his masculinity, and his affection firsthand for a span of days, then encapsulate it to last her the rest of her life. No man could take Cooper's place. She knew that. She also knew she could not, *would* not live the life of a military wife. It would lead to misery for them both.

She knew now that she hadn't reckoned enough with the pain she'd feel, that Cooper might feel, when she said goodbye. She hadn't expected that knowledge to hurt and shame her this much.

Now was the time to tell him. She'd used him enough.

"Cooper, we have to talk."

"Yes, I know, but later. Now, let's find that buried treasure. Time is running out."

Her lips numbed. Time *was* running out.

He gave her a quick peck on the mouth, then reached for his shovel, which he'd left leaning against the wall. "Let's go find some mayonnaise jars."

Swamped with guilt and self-loathing, Paige felt trapped.

"Come on!" Cooper called as he strode away to dig for the money she needed.

Venting a ragged sigh, Paige took up her shovel and followed him.

Eight hours later she stepped out of what seemed like the millionth hole to find Cooper leaning on his shovel, staring into the distance.

"Have you thought of something?" she asked, taking a swig from her glass of water.

"That shed."

She blinked. "What?"

"Next to that last greenhouse. That shed. There's a pile of bags in it."

"Yes. The tree fern."

"How long has it been there?"

"The bags?" Paige went very still as she caught the reasoning behind his questions. "We've kept the tree fern there for years."

Cooper grinned. "C'mon."

They removed from the shed the plastic barrel in which Paige stored the sphagnum moss, and six lightweight bags of tree fern. Then they set about excavating.

Paige was the first to shatter a mayonnaise jar. Then Cooper. And between them they carefully uncovered four more.

Her fingers trembling, she picked the rolls of twenty dollar bills from broken glass and counted. As the amount grew, so did her excitement. He began to count aloud with her. When they reached what was needed to pay off the taxes, she whooped with joy.

"Cooper! We've done it!" She leaped up and waved the wad of money in her hand. "There's more than enough to pay the county. And look! There are still three more jars!"

Laughing, he grabbed her and waltzed her through the dusk, barely avoiding the holes that peppered the ground. They danced until they were breathless. Finally they stopped, gasping for air, still in their dancers' embrace.

As their playfulness faded and their labored breathing eased, awareness sharpened between them. Tension prickled through Paige, deepening into her muscles, pressing against her lungs. She could feel Cooper's arms tighten slightly, the hard sinews in his body shifting as he drew her closer.

Slowly, almost against her will, she lifted her face to meet his gaze. Twilight veiled the rich golden color of his eyes, but she knew it as well as she knew the hue of her own. She found she couldn't look away.

When he spoke, his voice was low and intense.

"Marry me."

Chapter Eleven

The blood drained from Paige's face. She felt the numbness of shock spreading through her body.

No! This wasn't supposed to happen! She'd been so careful not to tell him she loved him, not to lead him on about a future they might share.

But he'd told her he loved her, and apparently she'd failed in concealing her love for him. For someone as honorable as Cooper, apparently love meant commitment.

His every action had proclaimed his feelings for her, from his heart-melting smile to his asking his father for help. For her.

And she loved him for it. She loved Cooper Angelsmith and all his little ways, and all his little quirks. She loved his generosity, and his warm strength, and his humor.

She wanted to marry him. More than anything in the world, she wanted to be his wife.

But she couldn't. If she weakened now, they might both suffer for years to come.

Paige wanted to be Cooper's wife, and his wife alone.

Not a Navy wife. Not an Army wife. Not a Marine Corps wife.

She wasn't opposed to helping a man with his career. Unless that career possessed him, leaving her the third party out. The one left behind. To pace the halls and mark off the days... and wonder.

"Well?" he prompted, smiling. "Say yes. Marry me, Paige."

"I... can't."

Silence pulsed between them.

His smile faded. "Can't?"

She avoided his eyes.

"Can't?" he repeated more forcefully. "After what we've been through? What we've shared?" His gaze focused on her like a laser. "I think I deserve to know your reason, don't you?"

"I gave you my reason in California. You're in the military."

He dropped his arms from around her, and she shivered, feeling suddenly exposed and vulnerable... and alone.

In the twilight, Cooper's face hardened. "I thought— *look at me!*"

Reluctantly she met his gaze.

He continued, his voice low and savage. "Things changed between us. *We* changed. Are you denying that?"

She shook her head, unable to manage words. He was right. So right.

"I love you, Paige. And I know you love me."

She stared at him, numb with misery.

He studied her face for a long moment.

Finally he drew a sharp breath and released it. "I've been such a fool." He lifted his face to the darkened sky and closed his eyes. "God, I've been such a blind fool."

His self-ridicule hurt her more than rightfully casting blame on her ever could. She felt him closing himself off from her, and it tore at her heart.

He turned on his heel and strode toward the house, and she knew he intended to leave for Jacksonville tonight. She also knew he had no money, no transportation.

"Wait!"

He stopped.

Paige scooped up a roll of twenty-five twenty dollar bills and ran to press it into his hands. "Please take this. At least—" her throat closed. She dragged in air in a long, shuddering breath. "At least let me keep my promise to finance the trip." The tears that splashed down her cheeks were hot and salty.

His eyes narrowed as he looked at the money he held. The muscles in his jaw worked. He didn't want the money, she could see that. She knew he had no choice but to take it. And she knew that made it worse for him.

He hesitated, then with a chopped nod, he rammed the bills into his pocket and stalked off.

"Cooper!"

He halted abruptly, but did not turn back to face her.

She had to say the words, to let him know he'd been right, even though it couldn't change things. "Cooper... I love you."

"Apparently," he answered hoarsely, "that's not enough."

When she straggled into the house twenty minutes later, he was gone.

Black fury seethed through Cooper as he glared unseeing out the backseat window of the taxi. He worked on it, fed it. Anger was easier to handle than the other things he felt. It was more familiar. Less...painful.

The cab pulled up to the curb at the departure level and he got out. He paid the driver, then picked up his suitcase and strode into the airline terminal. He stepped into line at the appropriate ticket counter and made it through the transaction by rote.

He'd have to fly into Charlotte, North Carolina, where he'd change planes and continue on to Jacksonville. It would be more than four hours before he reached his destination. Four hours, most of which would be spent crammed into a crowded airplane.

He wanted to be alone to curse and grieve.

He had hoped to make this leg of his journey with Paige by his side. She would have been talking about their upcoming wedding. He would have been planning their honeymoon. They would have returned to Camp Pendleton together, ready to share their lives.

Well, she'd made it clear she didn't want to share his life. She hadn't even needed time to consider his proposal.

I can't.

He swore under his breath, his oath harsh and vivid. Can't? Never had he met a woman more capable of coping with the demands placed on a marine's wife. Why, she was a regular little trooper. Brave. Feisty.

And unwilling.

His stomach knotted.

As he headed toward his gate, a cold loneliness filled him. He was tired of marching through life alone.

A four-lane street ran in front of what had once been Cooper's Classics. Now the showroom stood empty, one of the plate glass windows already marred by a BB shot, a large For Sale: Commercial Property sign taped on the inside. A light summer breeze sent an ice cream wrapper skittering across the vacant parking lot to flatten against a

wall of the large aluminum warehouse that had sheltered
the machine shop, garage, and supply depot. The place had
been alive with a cacophony of pneumatic drills, gunned
engines and the good-natured banter of mechanics.

The only sound on the premises today was moaning
caused by an occasional gust through eaves and cracks.

All the excitement of creation, the long hours and hard
work had come to this.

"The property will bring a good price, Nathe. That'll
give us each a tidy nest egg. It's really grown up around
here. When did they four-lane this street?"

"Last year, just after that shopping center went up."

Cooper nodded.

"I don't want anything from the sale of the property."
Nathan held up his hand, forestalling Cooper's objec-
tions, and continued. "I didn't put any of my money into
it, and I drew a decent salary for three years. In fact, I'd say
I was overpaid."

"We've been over this already, Nathe."

Several seconds passed. Cars sped by the two brothers.
The wrapper danced away to settle against the tall chain-
link fence.

"I'm sorry," Nathan said softly.

Cooper turned to look at his brother. Like Cooper, the
younger man had inherited their father's height and hair
color, but there the resemblance stopped. Nathan had been
endowed with the chocolate brown of their mother's eyes.

He rested his hand on Nathan's shoulder and gave a
commiserating squeeze. "So am I. I should have helped
you more. If I had, I would have seen this coming." He
wished he'd never had to leave Jacksonville and Cooper's
Classics. He'd expected too much of a twenty-two-year-old
graduate of Annapolis with a degree in political science

Now his brother was twenty-five and already haunted by the ghost of failure.

As if reading Cooper's thoughts the younger man shook his head as he gazed at the empty buildings. "I've never been good at the nuts and bolts of business. Not like you are. But you made me a partner because you couldn't be here. You trusted me and I blew it."

"No. *We* blew it. My only question is why you didn't call me as soon as you saw you were in trouble. I could have helped you."

"You've always helped me. Everybody in the family's always helped me. Don't you see? *I hate being the younger son.*"

Cooper frowned. He turned to face Nathan and found the hopelessness of years of frustration in the depths of dark eyes.

"You wanted to be a marine," Cooper said slowly as realization dawned.

"Yes."

"Then why didn't you go in from Annapolis?"

Nathan drew a sharp breath and released it as a long sigh. He fixed his gaze in the distance. "Because *you* had already gone in. You'd sacrificed your gift for the sake of our family's tradition. Could I do less when you asked me to run Classics?"

Cooper stared at him. "Gift?"

Now it was Nathan's turn to frown. "Good Lord, Coop, you're a business whiz. You seem to have a sixth sense. I've never seen anyone get as big a kick out of wheeling and dealing as you do. And you do it so well. But you gave it up without a complaint to become a marine, as tradition dictated. It was expected."

Cooper blinked. He hadn't complained because it had never occurred to him. From birth he'd been taught his destiny was tied to the Marine Corps. His world had always been encompassed by the military. It had never occurred to him to think he might be happier doing something else. He'd been too well indoctrinated into accepting his role in Angelsmith tradition to realize he had a choice.

As long as you chose your career.

Paige's words came back to him now. When she'd spoken them, they had irritated him more than they should have. He had flinched away from examining why.

"My God," Nathan said, searching his brother's face with concerned eyes, "you didn't even know."

No, that wasn't quite true, Cooper thought. He'd been aware of how much more satisfaction he'd received from Classics than he'd derived from his military career. But he'd assumed that's how it was supposed to be. When he retired after twenty or thirty years in the Marine Corps he could go on to indulge in something that excited him. He'd planned to expand Classics, or open another business.

He wasn't sure he wanted to wait another twenty or so years to try again.

"I'm a competent marine," he told Nathan, considering each word, "but I'm an inspired entrepreneur." And suddenly, as if he'd had to first acknowledge it in words, he knew it was true.

Color flagged Nathan's cheeks. "I'm not even a competent entrepreneur. But," he continued emphatically, "I know I could be a damned good marine."

Gradually, Cooper grinned and, to his relief and delight, his brother finally grinned back.

"What do you think we should do about it?" Cooper asked, his grin turning wicked.

Nathan rolled his eyes as they walked back to his car parked on the street. "Dad's not going to like this." But the younger man's smile didn't diminish.

"Oh, I don't know." Cooper slid into the seat and pulled the door closed. "He's not the bogeyman he'd like people to think he is."

Nathan looked skeptical.

"And since you're so eager to be a bad-ass marine," Cooper continued, "you can be the one to tell him."

Clay pots of orchid plants, studded with exotic blossoms in vibrant colors, hung from metal rods that ran the width of the greenhouse, suspended just under the roof. More plants cloaked the orderly rows of benches in shades of green studded here and there with fantastic jewellike blooms. The flowers imparted a fragrance so hauntingly sweet, so piercingly delicate it continued to elude accurate replication by man.

"Staring off into space again, I see."

Paige blinked and turned to find Waldo standing next to her.

"I thought you were coming to join me and Maggie for lunch."

"I'm sorry, Waldo. I got, uh, busy."

He eyed her hands, empty except for a key chain. She fingered the small brown stone. "Yeah," he agreed. "I can see that."

She flushed and changed the subject, hoping to avoid the familiar lecture. "Is lunch already prepared?"

"It is. And nobody makes a peanut butter sandwich like my wife."

Paige smiled. Since he and Maggie had married two months ago, right after his release from the hospital, Waldo never lost an opportunity to refer to her as "my wife."

Waldo had moved into Maggie's house and Paige was back to living alone. She'd assured the worried newlyweds she was happy that way.

"Do you mind if I pass up lunch today, Waldo?" she asked. "I'm not feeling very hungry. I'm sorry."

Waldo snorted. "You're sorry, all right. You've been sorry ever since you chased that marine off. Good fella, Maggie tells me. Thought a lot of you. And it's become clear to me that you think a lot of him." He took both her hands in his. "Call him back, missy. Call him back now. It's only been two months. It's not too late."

The painful misery that had filled Paige since the night Cooper had left finally became too much for her. A broken sob escaped her tightened throat. "Yes it is! It's t-too late."

Awkwardly, Waldo took her into his arms. "Tell me."

How could she explain her feelings when they'd tangled into such a confused mess? Two months ago she'd been determined not to live life alone, fretting and worrying about a man sent away by his duty. She hadn't wanted to be like her mother, pacing moonlit rooms and halls in lonely silence, waiting for her man to come home. A married woman made single yet still bound by her vows of fidelity and honor.

For the past eight weeks Paige had been unable to eat or sleep properly. She avoided mirrors, not wanting to see the mockery of dark circles and concave cheeks. She spent her nights restlessly walking through the house, sifting through her memories of a man she'd finally sent away. A man who'd offered to share with her those vows of fidelity and honor. A man she loved.

"Life as a military wife couldn't be any worse than life without Cooper at all," she said unevenly. She pressed her lips together to still their trembling. A second later she tried again. "I love him so much, Waldo."

He gently patted her back. "I know you do, missy. I know you do."

"I called his number at Camp Pendleton."

"And?"

"He's not there anymore."

"Well, what about a letter? They'd forward it to him at his next duty station."

"I wrote. No answer. And who can blame him? Who wants a crazy woman with a hamster?"

A rich, familiar baritone sounded from the doorway of the greenhouse. "I do."

Paige's head snapped up. She stared at the man who stood in the entrance. Her heartbeat quickened into an uncertain, frantic rhythm. Oxygen became scarce. Her world telescoped to that small section of the greenhouse. Vaguely, she was aware of Waldo withdrawing.

"You do?" Her voice sounded small and uncertain to her.

Cooper nodded, his face unreadable.

She flung herself across the short distance that separated them and into his arms. "Oh, Cooper, I was wrong! Anything's better than a future without you."

He held her tightly and she felt his heart pounding in his chest. He laughed raggedly. "I'm glad you feel that way."

After a long moment, Paige noticed the small cage sitting on the ground next to Cooper's right foot. "What have you brought?"

Cooper smiled sheepishly. "A lady friend for Henry. A bachelor's life isn't all it's cracked up to be."

They both regarded the petite ball of black and white fluff that refused to budge from her nest of wood shavings, presenting them with a view of her back.

"I think they're temperamentally suited, don't you?"

Paige felt torn between laughter and tears.

"I tried to call you," she managed, trying to absorb the reality of his presence, finding reassurance in his solid embrace. "They told me you weren't there anymore, but they wouldn't tell me where you'd gone."

"I'm here."

She nuzzled into the warmth of his throat. Under her cheek she felt the strong beat of his pulse. She smiled, knowing her own kept a similar pace. "I can see that. How long can you stay?"

When he didn't answer, she asked again, thinking he hadn't heard her. "How long can you stay?"

"As long as you want me to."

She lifted her head to look up at him, a small questioning frown tugging at her brows. Uncertain, she tested the waters. "I want you to stay forever."

Suddenly a glorious smile illuminated his face, and she knew why his name was Angelsmith.

"Sweetheart, I was hoping you'd say that." He framed her face between his palms and claimed her mouth with his.

The kiss was deep and hot and sublime, a crazy mixture of sexual and spiritual, a carnal communing that left them breathless and awed and hungry for more.

"I resigned my commission," he said.

Paige's eyes flew up to meet his. "Not for me. Please, Cooper, get it back. I'll be a marine's wife. I'll—I'll probably like it."

He chuckled. "No, you wouldn't. You'd hate it. But that's not why I resigned."

"It's not?"

"No." A smile curved that wonderful mouth as he brushed a tendril of hair back from her forehead. "I regret to say, the military isn't my true calling."

"You regret it?"

"Of course. The Marine Corps is a part of me. It's my heritage and, up until a few weeks ago, it's been my life. But I guess at heart I'm just a merchant."

"Just a merchant? There is no such thing. A *business person* has to be a market analyst, a strategist, and above all, a risk-taker." She smiled up at him. "I guess you just qualified for that last part."

He dropped a kiss on the tip of her nose. "I guess I did."

She opened her hand to reveal the key chain he had given her.

He smiled. "The desert rose. You kept it."

"Always." She stroked its rough surface with a fingertip. The past two months without Cooper had seemed like a desert at its worst—bleak and desolate. Now she felt alive again, filled with her love for him.

"How does your family feel about your decision to become a full-time entrepreneur?" she asked.

"Mom was pleased. Dad wasn't happy, but I think he's trying to understand. And Nathan..." He grinned. "Nathan has joined the Corps. Seems he's always wanted to be a marine."

"So the tradition continues."

"Slightly altered, but basically intact. And who knows? Maybe our firstborn child will want to be a marine."

Children. Paige smiled. Beautiful, amber-eyed children.

"Or a horticulturist," she countered.

"Hmm," he murmured, lowering his face to hers. "I can see this is going to take a lot of consideration. But first we have to make those babies."

"I told you, Angelsmith, I'm not into one-night stands," she quipped softly, her lips barely touching his.

"What about a cheap fling?"

She raised an eyebrow consideringly. "How cheap?"

"Whatever the going rate is for a blood test, a license, and a justice of the peace."

Surrounded by hundreds of fragrant blooms, they shared a kiss that pledged their love for the years to come.

*   *   *   *   *

Silhouette ❤ *Romance*®

COMING NEXT MONTH

#868 DIAMONDS ARE FOREVER—Linda Varner
Written in the Stars
Jeweler Thomas Wright was in the business of making wedding rings for *other* people. But the fascinating Jilly Sullivan soon had the hard-to-catch Gemini putting his designs on her.

#869 FATHER GOOSE—Marie Ferrarella
Police officer Del Santini never thought of becoming a dad—until he delivered Melissa Ryan's baby. Now he couldn't *stop* thinking of the single mom and her child . . . or stop loving them.

#870 THE RIGHT MAN FOR LOVING—Kristina Logan
When former childhood rivals Elizabeth Palmer and Michael Stafford competed for a coveted amusement park advertising account, they had no idea they'd end up in the tunnel of love. . . .

#871 GOODY TWO-SHOES—Vivian Leiber
Nobody could be as innocent as Sabrina Murray, and columnist Drew Carlson set out to prove it. Problem was, he *couldn't*—not unless he acted on the sizzling attraction between them.

#872 HIS FATHER'S HOUSE—Elizabeth Krueger
Five years ago, accused of a crime he didn't commit, Briant McCullough left town—and Samantha Barrister. Now he's back—to clear his reputation and reclaim the only woman he's ever loved. . . .

#873 ALONE AT LAST—Rita Rainville
Social worker Katie Donovan needed time for herself. But sexy contractor Judd Jordan was out to convince her that, while being alone was fine—being *together* was better.

AVAILABLE THIS MONTH:

#862 ROOKIE DAD
Pepper Adams

#863 LONE STAR MAN
Dorsey Kelley

#864 MISSY'S PROPOSITION
Maris Soule

#865 GOING MY WAY
Terri Lindsey

#866 PALACE CITY PRINCE
Arlene James

#867 ANGEL AT LARGE
Peggy Webb

The spirit of motherhood is the spirit of love—and how
better to capture that special feeling than in our short story
collection...

Curtiss Ann Matlock
Carole Halston
Linda Shaw

Three glorious new stories that embody the very essence of
family and romance are contained in this heartfelt tribute to
Mother. Share in the joy by joining us and three of your
favorite Silhouette authors for this celebration of
motherhood and romance.

Available at your favorite retail outlet in May.

"GET AWAY FROM IT ALL" SWEEPSTAKES

HERE'S HOW THE SWEEPSTAKES WORKS

NO PURCHASE NECESSARY

To enter each drawing, complete the appropriate Official Entry Form or a 3" by 5" index card by hand-printing your name, address and phone number and the trip destination that the entry is being submitted for (i.e., Caneel Bay, Canyon Ranch or London and the English Countryside) and mailing it to: Get Away From It All Sweepstakes, P.O. Box 1397, Buffalo, New York 14269-1397.

No responsibility is assumed for lost, late or misdirected mail. Entries must be sent separately with first class postage affixed, and be received by: 4/15/92 for the Caneel Bay Vacation Drawing, 5/15/92 for the Canyon Ranch Vacation Drawing and 6/15/92 for the London and the English Countryside Vacation Drawing. Sweepstakes is open to residents of the U.S. (except Puerto Rico) and Canada, 21 years of age or older as of 5/31/92.

For complete rules send a self-addressed, stamped (WA residents need not affix return postage) envelope to: Get Away From It All Sweepstakes, P.O. Box 4892, Blair, NE 68009.

© 1992 HARLEQUIN ENTERPRISES LTD.

SWP-RLS

- -

"GET AWAY FROM IT ALL" SWEEPSTAKES

HERE'S HOW THE SWEEPSTAKES WORKS

NO PURCHASE NECESSARY

To enter each drawing, complete the appropriate Official Entry Form or a 3" by 5" index card by hand-printing your name, address and phone number and the trip destination that the entry is being submitted for (i.e., Caneel Bay, Canyon Ranch or London and the English Countryside) and mailing it to: Get Away From It All Sweepstakes, P.O. Box 1397, Buffalo, New York 14269-1397.

No responsibility is assumed for lost, late or misdirected mail. Entries must be sent separately with first class postage affixed, and be received by: 4/15/92 for the Caneel Bay Vacation Drawing, 5/15/92 for the Canyon Ranch Vacation Drawing and 6/15/92 for the London and the English Countryside Vacation Drawing. Sweepstakes is open to residents of the U.S. (except Puerto Rico) and Canada, 21 years of age or older as of 5/31/92.

For complete rules send a self-addressed, stamped (WA residents need not affix return postage) envelope to: Get Away From It All Sweepstakes, P.O. Box 4892, Blair, NE 68009.

© 1992 HARLEQUIN ENTERPRISES LTD.

SWP-RLS

"GET AWAY FROM IT ALL"

Brand-new Subscribers-Only Sweepstakes

OFFICIAL ENTRY FORM

This entry must be received by: May 15, 1992
This month's winner will be notified by: May 31, 1992
Trip must be taken between: June 30, 1992—June 30, 1993

YES, I want to win the Canyon Ranch vacation for two. I understand the prize includes round-trip airfare and the two additional prizes revealed in the BONUS PRIZES insert.

Name _____

Address _____

City _____

State/Prov._____ Zip/Postal Code_____

Daytime phone number _____
(Area Code)

Return entries with invoice in envelope provided. Each book in this shipment has two entry coupons — and the more coupons you enter, the better your chances of winning!
© 1992 HARLEQUIN ENTERPRISES LTD.   2M-CPN

"GET AWAY FROM IT ALL"

Brand-new Subscribers-Only Sweepstakes

OFFICIAL ENTRY FORM

This entry must be received by: May 15, 1992
This month's winner will be notified by: May 31, 1992
Trip must be taken between: June 30, 1992—June 30, 1993

YES, I want to win the Canyon Ranch vacation for two. I understand the prize includes round-trip airfare and the two additional prizes revealed in the BONUS PRIZES insert.

Name _____

Address _____

City _____

State/Prov._____ Zip/Postal Code_____

Daytime phone number _____
(Area Code)

Return entries with invoice in envelope provided. Each book in this shipment has two entry coupons — and the more coupons you enter, the better your chances of winning!
© 1992 HARLEQUIN ENTERPRISES LTD.   2M-CPN